GOTHIC GHOST STORIES:
AN EXERCISE IN HORROR

To: Victoria,

Best wishes

Dot x x

October 2021

## Also by the author

*Ten for the Devil*
*The Coast to Coast Walk*

# Gothic Ghost Stories

## AN EXERCISE IN HORROR

TREVOR K BELL

The Book Guild Ltd

First published in Great Britain in 2021 by
The Book Guild Ltd
9 Priory Business Park
Wistow Road, Kibworth
Leicestershire, LE8 0RX
Freephone: 0800 999 2982
www.bookguild.co.uk
Email: info@bookguild.co.uk
Twitter: @bookguild



Typeset in 11.6pt Adobe Garamond Pro

Printed on FSC accredited paper
Printed and bound in Great Britain by 4edge Limited

ISBN 978 1913551 889

British Library Cataloguing in Publication Data.
A catalogue record for this book is available from the British Library.

This book is dedicated to M.R.James,
master ghost story writer.

# Contents

# The Haunted Train Set

It was in 1972, at the time of the Treasures of Tutankhamun Exhibition at the British Museum, when Mr Silverdale looked in at the window of the model hobby shop, not far from Kings Cross Station, and his eyes nearly popped out of his head. What he saw was an A4 4-6-2 class 'Streak' locomotive, with Kings X emblazoned in white between the front buffers, designating the London station from which the Streak had previously operated. The engine was resplendent in the apple-green livery of the Northern Line, and boasted a full set of red and cream coaches. Mr Silverdale looked at the set with the same adoration he might have shown upon seeing Aphrodite for the first time.

'How much?' he asked, as nonchalantly as he could, entering the shop and pointing to the Northern Line locomotive in the window.

Mr Jenkins, the hobby shop proprietor, was a shrewd salesman and knew his type of client well. The Streak was a rarity in the collectors' world, particularly one in this condition, and he meant to extract every penny he could from his prospective purchaser.

'Oh, several hundred pounds, I should think,' answered Jenkins, casually, taking the locomotive from the window and setting it up on the display rail on the counter, moving the engine backwards and forwards to catch Mr Silverdale's eye, 'particularly one in this condition with a full set of carriages.'

Mr Silverdale's hands dived defensively into his pockets.

'As a matter of fact,' Jenkins continued, not taking his eyes off the engine, 'a gentleman, not five minutes before you arrived, sir, came in to look at it and said he had to have it at any price. An American gentleman, I think he was, sir, if I'm not much mistaken.' He glanced out of the window, as if he were expecting the prospective purchaser to return at any moment, trying to intimidate Mr Silverdale. 'I'm convinced he'll be back for it in the morning, if not earlier,' he said, glancing at Mr Silverdale, who frowned at the prospect of the engine crossing the Atlantic. 'These Americans have too much money, in my opinion,' continued Jenkins, shrugging his shoulders, 'but business is business, and with respect to yourself, sir, a bird in the hand is worth more than two in the bush, as you might say. But I'll favour you on this occasion. If you can take it today, sir, the Streak's yours!' And with that, he stood back, allowing the enthusiast himself to impel the engine along the rail, knowing he had this particular fish well and truly hooked. To Mr Silverdale, the thought of anyone else owning the puffer was abhorrent. He was highly patriotic and this engine was English; therefore, it should remain in Blighty, but he was frightened of the sum he would have to pay.

'Anyway,' put in Jenkins, after a few moments had gone by, thinking he might have pitched his price too high. 'To be honest' – which he wasn't – 'I'd rather sell it to an Englishman than to an American, so I'll slit my own throat and say two hundred and fifty pounds, and it's yours.'

Mr Silverdale gulped. It was still a considerable sum of money.

'Incidentally,' said Jenkins, turning the screw, 'regarding provenance, I was told by the seller that this train once ran on the model railway of George Hudson himself, the Railway King, and the real Streak locomotive is running north from King's later today!'

'Really!' said Mr Silverdale, with genuine surprise, still impelling the locomotive along the display track, but with the increasing suspicion he was being manipulated. Coming more to his senses, he declared, cannily, 'One hundred and seventy-five pounds is all I can manage, I'm afraid.'

Jenkins fingered his lips thoughtfully, sucking air in through his teeth to indicate what a hard bargain Mr Silverdale was driving. 'Very well, sir, two hundred pounds and it's yours,' and he slapped his hand down on the table.

Mr Silverdale felt helpless. 'Okay,' he said, 'I hope you'll take a cheque?'

'I suppose so,' said the shopkeeper, with a deep sigh, as if he had mortally wounded himself by lowering the price. He went into the rear of the shop, boxed up the locomotive and carriages, then handed it to his customer, pleased with his profit of seventy pounds. The doorbell jangled and Mr Silverdale left the shop with his train set, closing the door behind him.

Jenkins, going again into the rear of the shop, enthusiastically declared to his wife, 'The Streak's sold, thank God!'

His wife turned from the table to face him, dusting the flour off her arms and going over to the teapot. 'Well, I *am* glad,' she said, pouring out two cups. 'This calls for a celebration! There's been no peace since that thing came into the house. Such a feeling of dread it gave me, just to look at that locomotive. Evil, that's what it was, *evil.*' And she made the sign of a cross to ward off any malignant spirit that might attach itself to her simply by the mention of it. The shop bell rang again and Mr Jenkins went out to serve a new customer.

His business concluded, Mr Silverdale set off briskly to King's Cross Station, the train set under his arm, to travel, coincidentally, along the same line on which the Streak had originally run from King's Cross to his home in Hitchin. The journey was uneventful, and Mr Silverdale alighted from the train as usual, at Hitchin.

Immediately upon arriving home, he unpacked the engine and its carriages and set it running along the rails of his model railway. Round and round it flew, in a dizzying enchantment, Mr Silverdale imaginatively in the cab of the engine, driving it past the shunting yard, between the houses – where the lines ran under a bridge – through various cuttings and along by the river. He saw himself waving to all the people who populated his model railway. The very best thing, from his point of view, was that the real Hitchin Station, onto whose platform he had so recently alighted, and upon which station his own station had been so carefully modelled, could be seen through his very own bedroom window. And now there was the possibility of seeing his model engine, and the real Streak, together, this very day! He was so enraptured with the prospect, that he forgot to eat his dinner, playing with his locomotive until well after dusk; in fact, until the lights of the real Hitchin Station came on and shone through his un-curtained window.

* * *

But our story now takes a twist. Curiously, in London, later that same day, three hours after Mr Silverdale had purchased his Streak locomotive from Mr Jenkins, a Mr Glimmer, whose home lay in Huntingdon, a little further along the track from Mr Silverdale's home in Hitchin, had obtained an acquisition of his own; namely, a talisman which had recently been adorning the neck of Tutankhamun's mummy, lying in a glass-topped display case in the Egyptian section of the British Museum. Mr Glimmer was a great admirer of the mummy, but not for aesthetic reasons, for it was not the first time he had visited its display case. Indeed, he had previously made a wax impression of the key, which had been inadvertently left in the lock by a guard, for the purpose of stealing the talisman. This key he now inserted into the lock, determined to take the mummy's talisman from around its neck. He did not notice, as he took it, that the stone statue of Tutankhamun turned ten degrees towards him, though it is true that a queer feeling came over him at that same moment. He glanced furtively around, expecting to see one of the museum's guards approaching, though he saw no-one.

He now turned the key in the lock and saw the lid rise. Unfastening the trinket from around the mummy's neck, he slipped it into his pocket, quietly closing the lid. We do not know why the alarm did not sound, but it did not, and his anticipated run to the exit became a leisurely stroll. In a further stroke of luck, the theft was not discovered until well after closing time, and as the guard had an urgent appointment that evening, he irresponsibly decided to leave the reporting of the theft until the following morning.

Yet it was also the case that, in the course of removing the talisman from around the mummy's neck, its hand had come up and had caught Mr Glimmer's own. It was thinner than a human hand, without muscle or sinew, yet it seemed to exert a powerful force on his own hand, as if it were trying to retain possession of the talisman. Afterwards, irritated by the mummy's touch, Mr Glimmer took out his handkerchief, spat upon it and wiped it. I suppose a more sensitive man might have taken this as a warning to return the trinket to its owner; however, having secured his prize, he hardly gave it a second thought as he proceeded to King's Cross Station where he must catch his train home. He showed his return ticket at the barrier and walked along the platform to where the 'Falcon', also a Streak locomotive, was waiting, steam hissing from its wheel-cylinders. It was pulling exactly the same number of carriages as the model engine currently making circuits of Mr Silverdale's bedroom. Mr Glimmer looked over his shoulder, to make sure he was not being pursued, and stepped on board.

As he did so, the conductor, thinking a small child had also brushed past him, without presenting a ticket, asked, 'Is he with you, sir?'

'Who?' said Mr Glimmer, turning back to look at the conductor, from the carriage. 'There's no-one with me.'

Doubting his senses, the conductor went so far as to board the train, to check Mr Glimmer's word, but he saw no small child, either on the train or on the platform.

'I could have sworn!' he muttered, tilting his cap back and scratching his forehead, 'that a little black boy was with you, sir.' And, for the rest of the day, the conductor was aware of the smell of something ancient and pungent in his nostrils, which caused him to continually blow his nose in an attempt to rid himself of the aroma. Eventually, he persuaded himself he had been mistaken. But the aroma persisted.

Soon the guard blew his whistle and the train set off through Potters Bar, Hatfield and on towards Hitchin, along the same route the Streak had taken in former days.

Mr Glimmer settled himself into an empty compartment in the carriage immediately behind the engine, taking a seat by the window, sitting with his back to the engine. When the other passengers had settled into their carriages, he found himself alone,. He carefully took out the talisman from his handkerchief. The gold of the trinket winked at him in the car lights. Closely examining the talisman, he saw that Anubis and Osiris, the gods of the underworld, were holding on to the legs of a man-like figure. Underneath them, the god Bast (daughter of Ra) was attempting to put out the flames which threatened to rise and incinerate the constrained figure. Above all, Hanhet,

God of Eternity, was pulling on the figure's arms in an effort to counteract the efforts of Anubis and Osiris pulling from below. The depiction, according to Mr Glimmer's research, indicated that the talisman showed the battle for a man's soul after death. For he had come to believe that, if Bast could put out the fire, and Hanhet could lift the figure up into eternity, the owner of the talisman might also receive such assistance and be lifted up into eternity. Furthermore, his research suggested that the talisman possessed magical properties; namely, that it bestowed long life and good fortune on the wearer, and he foresaw for himself a golden future.

As the train rattled north, he continued to gloat over his possession, imagining the benefits that would accrue to him now that it was in his possession. He *knew* his health and fortune would begin to improve; he *knew* he would feel a greater sense of permanence in the scheme of things; he *knew* he would feel physically and mentally invigorated. Indeed it seemed to him that he was not far from immortality itself as he returned the talisman to his handkerchief and then to his pocket. Everything he had ever desired, he thought, would shortly be his!

Soon the exciting day, the rocking of the train and the warmth of the compartment caused him to doze off, but it was not a restful doze. He dreamt that the mummy, from whom he had stolen the talisman, had suddenly come to life and, worse, was pursuing him for it. Now he recalled the feeling of the mummy's hand upon his own when he had first taken the trinket from the case. In his dream, he felt a strange presence in the carriage; as if he was not alone. The nightmare was so real that, shortly before Hatfield, he awoke in a state of acute anxiety, sweat running down his face and neck, as if he had actually been running away from the mummy. *What on earth?* he said to himself. *What's happening to me!*

* * *

Meanwhile, further up the line in Hitchin, Mr Silverdale was kneeling down beside the luggage van of his model train, examining a number of miniature mail sacks that had been installed there, when, on a whim, he inserted the index finger of his right hand to feel them. Almost immediately, he drew it back hastily, for it seemed to him as if something had – not stirred, perhaps – but yielded in an odd, live kind of way, in one of the sacks. Imagine his surprise when, in the course of removing his finger, a small dark figure wrapped in bandages came tumbling out onto the siding. Was it a casualty from a model hospital train that had mistakenly been placed in the luggage van of *his* model train? He did not think so. The figure looked more like an embalmed mummy, and it seemed to wriggle slightly. *What am I to do with this?* he asked himself, a deep sense of disquiet coming over him. He then had an idea. He had only one other passenger on the Streak, the one wearing a blue suit, who was sitting in the carriage immediately behind the engine, so he placed the little bandaged figure in a sitting position in the last carriage. Now he would have a passenger at each end of the train! This seemed to him to be a most equitable solution. Satisfied, he watched the train make a few more circuits of the track before switching off the power and retiring to bed. He did not draw his bedroom curtains for, if he was still awake, he wanted to have the opportunity of seeing both the model and the real Hitchin Station in view as the real Streak passed through. He hoped to catch sight of both, at one and the same time.

But he was not asleep for long.

Though there was no train due at Hitchin Station, on either the *up* or the *down* line at that time, it is undeniable that, two hours after he had fallen into the arms of Hypnos, Mr Silverdale was startled out of his slumber by the sound of a train whistle. Indeed, he was so much startled that, not only did he listen acutely for its repetition, but he sat bolt upright in his bed trying to determine from whence the sound had come, and why each carriage of the Streak was now illuminated. Most of all, he asked himself, why the Falcon of his model railway had set off along the track without the power being turned on, and why fifty or so more passengers had now seemingly joined the train; whereas, before, there had been only the man in the blue suit sitting in the carriage behind the engine, and the mummy seated in the last carriage. He also wanted to know why the whole of his model railway was now lit up; why the streetlamps were now all illuminated, and the lights were now shining from the windows of the houses. Perhaps, most of all, he wanted to know why, above his model station, he was no longer looking at the wall of his bedroom, but at an inky-blue night sky. 'How can all this be?' he asked himself.

In the next instant, he noticed that the mummy figure, which he had inserted into the last carriage of the train, had come to life and was moving stealthily, if erratically, along the train towards the carriage immediately behind the engine. The mummy did not look to the right or to the left as it proceeded towards the carriage and, astonishingly, the other passengers seemed not to notice it. It was as if the mummy figure was invisible to them. Unfortunately, the man in the blue suit, sitting behind the engine, would soon notice it.

When the mummy reached his carriage, it adopted a stooping posture, stretching out its arms towards the door. 'Was it blind?' The mummy felt for the compartment door, turned the handle and stepped inside. It came towards Mr Glimmer, its expression one of indescribable menace, its tongue darting forwards and back, like a snake. Had it tasted Mr Glimmer's scent? To his abject horror, Mr Glimmer recognised the figure as the mummy from whom he had stolen the talisman. It was at that instant that his nightmare had come true! He looked out of the window of his compartment: could he escape through there? No, it was too small! Surely there must be something he could do? In the next instant, he took the talisman from his pocket and held it out towards the mummy in hopeless entreaty. The mummy's smile broadened. In the next instant, with astonishing quickness, it sprang forward and clutched at Mr Glimmer's throat, its long fingernails penetrating his flesh.

At that precise moment the model train in Mr Silverdale's room stopped, all the lights in the carriages of the model train went out, and the room returned to normal. 'What now!' Mr Silverdale cried, wondering if his wits had left him altogether.

On an impulse, he went to his bedroom window and looked out. There he saw the real Streak locomotive pulling into the station. As it came to a halt, the guard shouted from the window of the train and there was quite a commotion on the platform. A carriage door (the one behind the engine) was flung open, and the man in the blue suit was taken out of the train and put onto a stretcher. He saw that the man in the blue suit was identical in all respects to the figure in his own model train. 'My God!' he exclaimed. 'I'm going mad! My model railway has turned into real life!'

* * *

The following day, Mr Silverdale read in his local paper that a Mr Glimmer, travelling on the Streak train from King's Cross to Sandy, had been found dead in his compartment as the train pulled in to Hitchin Station. The conductor, who had accompanied the train north, remembered that a man in a blue suit, whom he now understood to be Mr Glimmer, had boarded the train at King's Cross Station. He recalled how he thought a small black boy, the size of a pigmy, perhaps, had been travelling with the gentleman, whom he had seen leave

Mr Glimmer's carriage as the train had pulled in to Hitchin Station. He thought it was the same figure that had brushed past him at King's Cross.

When a doctor came to examine the man at the station, he pronounced him dead at the scene, and formed the opinion that Mr Glimmer had suffered a cardiac arrest. He could not be sure of the cause, though the man's face had retained an expression of such abject horror, that his eyes were wild and staring. The doctor noticed there were scratches and abrasions around the man's neck, indicative of being clawed by a wild animal, though he considered none of the flesh wounds had been fatal. A search of the train failed to reveal any creature capable of inflicting such injuries, either wild or domesticated, and the local press concluded that the man's death was rather mysterious. In a further twist, on the same evening, a Mrs Brown, whose house backed onto the railway south of Hitchin, watching out for the return home of her station porter husband through her bedroom window, shortly after the Streak had pulled in, said she had seen a small black figure running along the track in the direction of London's King's Cross. She shouted at the figure, as she knew it was dangerous to run along the railway, but the figure had continued along the rails in its own inimitable way.

* * *

At the British Museum, the following morning, the guard who had been in charge of the room where the mummy had been displayed, and from which the talisman had been stolen, reported the theft to his supervisor, but then noticed that the talisman had been mysteriously returned. The guard did not understand how this could have happened, as he knew the museum, as usual, was kept securely locked and guarded during the night. The supervisor's superiors did not know what to make of the guard's report but, after much discussion, it was decided that the guard must have imagined the whole thing and that the talisman had never gone missing in the first place. He was warned to be more careful in his reporting in future, and to report all theft immediately to the supervisor, or else face the prospect of immediate dismissal. In another oddity, the statue of Tutankhamun, which had turned to face the mummy's case at the time of the theft, had returned to its original position.

As for Mr Silverdale, understandably disconcerted by the incident, he subsequently began to develop an interest in model aeroplanes, swearing he would have nothing further to do with model trains and their carriages. As for Mr Jenkins, from whose hobby shop Mr Silverdale had purchased the locomotive, he refused absolutely to buy it back at any price, saying his wife would not allow its return on account of the fact that very unsettling things had happened in the house when the train set had been in their possession. Eventually, Mr Silverdale sold the train set, at a considerable loss, to an enthusiast from Hatfield who, while examining the mail car, subsequently noticed a Zulu-like figure fall out of one of the mail sacks, and he wondered if it did not wriggle slightly.

# Inside the House of the Dead

'I say, Tulip,' said a staffroom colleague to the Head of English at Blackstone Hall Public School, Oxfordshire, when they sat down together for lunch. 'I hear you're off to Weimar. Whatever makes you want to go to that place at *this* moment?' It was 1913 and there was talk of war brewing between Germany and England.

'Because it's the crucible of Germanic culture,' Tulip replied. 'And, I think, if we understood the Germans better, perhaps we wouldn't be thinking of battling them. Apart from that, Weimar is a beautiful medieval town at the heart of Thuringia, the home of several artistic and literary giants. Reason enough?'

His colleague grinned. 'A tin-pot fiefdom if you ask me!' he said, canvassing for a laugh. 'There are more attractive places to visit than Weimar, *and* it's full of Germans!' His effort was rewarded by a bout of giggling from around the table.

'I think you should go,' teased the art teacher. 'You could

enroll in the German army whilst you're there and practise your goose-stepping!'

Another bout of giggling.

The ribbing went on over lunch. Mr Tulip wisely held his peace and, the next day, being the end of term, he caught a train to the south coast. From there, he caught a ferry to Ostend in Belgium, then took a coach to Hamburg and a train to Berlin, arriving in Weimar in the late afternoon. Tardy in gathering all his belongings, the available taxis had gone by the time he disembarked and he was forced to trundle his small suitcase into the town, noting that many of the jostling pedestrians had guidebooks in their hands. *These are all cultural travellers like myself,* he thought. For just as English-people are drawn to Shakespeare and Stratford-Upon-Avon, German visitors to Weimar are even more aesthete pilgrims, feasting on the town's pantheon of artistic and intellectual saints such as Schiller, Sebastian Bach, and Johann Wolfgang von Goethe. As he approached the Herderplatz and Market districts, he marvelled at the medieval architecture. At the Schloss, where it is said a spurt of divine blood rains down in mercy from the beard of Lucas Cronach, his weary legs and empty stomach reminded him that he had yet to secure a hostelry for the night, and he began to investigate likely hotels.

Eschewing the famous Elephant Hotel, he settled for the more-modestly priced Thuringia Inn, as this had the advantage of being reasonably close to the town centre, and explained to the landlord that he would need a room for three weeks, his allotted time in Weimar. After a tour of the available rooms, he plumbed for a room on the ground floor. It had a number of beds and overlooked a small, if gloomy, courtyard and further benefited from having its own entrance, through which he could come and go as he pleased. The landlord explained that the room was sometimes used as a dormitory for visiting parties of schoolchildren, and the smaller room off to one side, with a single bed and a viewing window was for the visiting teacher to observe his charges. It also boasted its own bath, sink and toilet. It would serve as Mr Tulip's bathroom. Of a number of beds, in the larger room, he selected one in the right-hand corner – the one furthest from the internal door – as it benefitted from what little natural light shone through the five courtyard windows. He wondered if the pattern of the windows, which took the form of a cross, was meant to represent the Trinity, though the room was clearly not a religious building.

Finishing his unpacking, he ventured out to find a suitable restaurant for dinner, deciding on a convenient establishment not far from the Thuringia Inn. He settled down to enjoy a meal of sausages and potatoes, washing it down with a good hock. Satiated, he managed a further brief sally into the town before returning, rather tired, to his room, which, he now thought had an unpleasant atmosphere. After washing in the adjacent bathroom in the small room, he ran quickly to his bed and switched off the light, feeling an increasing sense of unease.

It was curious, therefore, that two hours after slipping unconscious, he was awakened by the sound of a tinkling bell, originating, he thought, from the opposite end of the room. Oddly, with the tinkling of the bell came an almost irrepressible desire to sneeze, just as if his nose was being tickled with a feather. Though he rubbed it vigorously, the tickling sensation persisted. To complete his irritation, the mattress he had previously thought so comfortable, now appeared to have acquired several lumps and bumps which seemed to constantly shift their position without any deliberate movement on his part. It was almost as if, sleeping beneath him, was a restless occupant. After a disturbed night, snatching what sleep he could, he sought out the landlord.

'Mr Spiegel!' shouted a grumpy Mr Tulip, coming through

into the bar, 'that mattress of yours is very uncomfortable. I hardly slept a wink on it all night. I can't spend another night on it as it is. The damn thing is all humps and hollows and seems to have a life of its own. You must make up a spare!'

The landlord, somewhat taken aback, frowned and turned towards him. 'It's the first time I've heard of it, sir. An uncomfortable mattress, you say? I've not had a complaint like that before.' He shrugged his shoulders but, firmly of the opinion that the customer was always right, said: 'Leave it to me, sir, I'll get the girl to change it for you.'

'And another thing,' said Mr Tulip, 'I kept hearing this tinkling bell all night, as if someone was ringing for the night porter. And my nose felt as if it was being continually tickled with a feather. I suppose it could have been a fly, but I couldn't hear or see any. And there's this most awful smell. I didn't notice it when I first moved in, but I do now. I suggest the room needs a good clean!'

Again, on the back foot, Mr Spiegel said:

'I'm sorry to hear you report such things, sir, but rest assured, I'll see these things attended to the moment you leave. What you report to me, sir, is a puzzle, but I'll see to everything. And now, if you'll excuse me, sir, I hope you have a pleasant day.' And with that, he sped up the stairs with a customer's tea-tray.

Satisfied that matters would be put right, Mr Tulip returned to his room, his nose wrinkling up at the bad smell. Shortly afterwards he went out through the gloomy courtyard into the town, rounding the corner of the Grünes Schloss to the house of Haus Stein, which had been the home of Goethe's first great love, Charlotte Stein. Returning to the Schloss, he examined copies of manuscripts by Goethe and Schiller, ascending the gilt-trimmed gallery, where he admired several busts of the great scholars of Weimar. Rapidly intoxicated by everything 'Weimar', he retreated to a leafy esplanade for respite and sat, slightly breathless, in the shade. He was glad the 'Philistines' at Blackstone Hall – as he liked to call them – were not with him to spoil this German Renaissance.

Yet, something was spoiling his pleasure, for, as he made his way from place to place, he felt a continuing tickling sensation in his nose, heard the tinkling bell earlier reported to the landlord, and his nose continued to be assaulted by a most awful odour. 'Can't all this stop!' he said to himself. 'Damn it all! Wasn't he entitled to some peace and quiet after a hard year's teaching?'

And so, Mr Tulip continued his tour, plagued by the unwelcome phenomena mentioned, and we join him in the early evening sipping coffee in a small restaurant, pondering his own philosophy of Weimar classicism. He agreed with Schiller about the need to acknowledge the reality of emotional experience, and about the inadequacy of a purely abstract psychology – but was unable to entertain the thought that knowledge was something separate and self-fulfilling. As a romantic, of course he admired the stories and poems of both Schiller and Goethe. Particularly in his teenage years, he had been enthralled by *The Bride of Messina*, *William Tell* and Goethe's *The Sorrows of Young Werther*.

Later that evening, at dinner, we find him seated at a quiet restaurant in the Herderplatz, sitting under a summer awning, leisurely perusing the menu. Choosing the daily 'special' of potato, bacon, beans and sausages, he ordered a bottle of red French wine. So far so good! But shortly after commencing his meal, the phenomena which had marred his enjoyment all day, again intruded; namely, the ringing of the bell, the tickling sensation, the awful smell, and so on. Except now, there seemed to be a shadow looming over him and, regardless of what position he adopted, it drew ever closer. The proprietor of the restaurant, keen to take his order and to know if Mr Tulip would be a repeat customer, asked him the name of the hotel at which he was staying. Mr Tulip told him; and, rather desperate for someone to verify his sensory experiences, broached the question of the ringing in his ears, the tickling sensation, and the bad odour.

'Can you hear that tinkling bell, landlord?' he asked eagerly. 'It's beginning to get on my nerves. The first time I heard it was in my room last night. It has been plaguing me ever since. Listen! Can you hear it? It's spoiling my enjoyment of Weimar. And there seems to be an awful smell and a shadow following me around.'

The proprietor cocked his head to one side and listened intently for a minute. 'A tinkling bell, you say…' he replied. 'I'm sorry, sir, I can only hear people talking and Joseph playing the accordion in the back room. A tinkling bell… how odd… how unusual!'

'Yes, and now there's this awful smell. I've never smelt anything like it… It's like the smell of a rotting corpse. Like the horrible smell of a mortuary. Surely you can smell it, landlord?'

The proprietor sniffed the air keenly, only to stare, blankly, back at Mr Tulip.

'I'm sorry, sir, I'm afraid I can't. A smell as well, you say? Begging your pardon, sir, perhaps you should consult a medical practitioner? These things may be coming from within, rather than out?'

Mr Tulip bristled and turned bright red, mortally offended at the insinuation that he was somehow losing his wits. He explained that there was nothing at all wrong with his senses, and no-one had ever made such a suggestion before. Would the landlord mind allowing him to finish his meal in peace, alone, and keep his opinions to himself!

'Of course, sir,' apologised the landlord. 'I'm sorry I spoke,' and he stepped across the pavement to serve another customer. Mr Tulip stared despondently into his wine glass. Perhaps he *was* going mad. On the other hand, perhaps all he needed was a good night's sleep. He hoped the landlord of the Thuringia Inn had cleaned his room and replaced the mattress.

Minutes later, when the time came to pay the bill, witnessing a partially recovered Mr Tulip, and wishing to restore the relationship with his customer, the landlord enquired: 'So you are staying at the Thuringia Inn, sir?'

'Yes, at the Thuringia Inn,' replied Mr Tulip, draining the last of his wine, avoiding the proprietor's gaze.

'I know it, sir. Rather tucked away in a dark corner.' He made a gesture of disapproval. 'Begging your pardon, sir, but it has a rather bad reputation I'm afraid.'

'A bad reputation?'

'Yes, sir, it has not always been a hotel. Customers staying there, who have dined here, have told me all sorts of tales. Tales about ghosts and the like. None of them pleasant, mainly on account of the fact that it wasn't always a hotel.'

'Not always a hotel?' said Mr Tulip. 'What do you mean?'

'A *leichenhauser*, sir. That's what it was. Local people won't stay there – knowing it was a *leichenhauser*.'

'A *leichenhauser*?'

'Yes, sir, a house where the dead were kept. A waiting mortuary.'

'A waiting mortuary?'

'Yes. A place where they placed the bodies to make sure a person had actually died. To make sure they *were* dead.'

'Good God! I've never heard of such a thing!'

'Oh, yes, sir, the dead were kept there for weeks sometimes. It was the first *leichenhauser* to be built in Germany, right here in Weimar. Christopher Hufeland, a local physician, an inhabitant of this city, built it.' The landlord proudly puffed out his chest, indicating his respect for the doctor who had established it.

'Well, I never!' said Mr Tulip.

'Yes, sir. They kept the bodies under surveillance day and

night, in case they come back to life. People at that time lived in morbid fear of being buried alive, so they prevailed upon their relatives to have themselves incarcerated in them. The room they used for the corpses was the very large one that overlooks the courtyard. *Leichenhausers* were established at the time Edgar Allen Poe, the American writer, wrote his story called *The Premature Burial.* Imagine the horror of being incarcerated in a coffin and hearing sods tumbling down on top of you. It sparked off a wave of fear in Germany about being buried alive. The tale caught their imaginations like a wildfire. The superintendent, the person in charge, would keep an eye on the corpses from the small room off to one side of the large room. It's a bathroom annexe to the main room now, I think, sir. In the large main room are still some of the original trestle-beds.'

Mr Tulip was taken aback. 'But that's the room where I'm sleeping! That's *my* room! Nobody's told me about it being a waiting mortuary!'

'Well, if you sleep there, sir,' the landlord said quietly, 'you sleep with the dead.' And he gave a short laugh to make light of what he had said.

Mr Tulip, struggling to compose himself, was unwilling to admit such things bothered him, so he paid the bill (without leaving a tip) and meandered slowly back to his room at the inn, pondering on what the proprietor of *The Young Werner* had said. As he was already aware of an unpleasant atmosphere in the room, he did not relish the prospect of entering it again.

Of course, we don't know if Mr Tulip had a premonition of what was about to happen next; except the hairs on the back of his neck began to stand erect. He listened intently at the door before stepping inside and flicking on the light. At the same instant, he saw something dart towards the bed in the far corner. 'What's that!?' he shouted involuntarily, his nerves on edge. How he wished, now, that he'd requested another bedchamber for the night, rather than asking the landlord to simply change the mattress. But it would not be possible to make such a request now; only if things proved not to have been done to his satisfaction. Pulling back the bedcovers he saw, alas the mattress had, indeed been changed and the bed made up with clean sheets. He sniffed the air. The unpleasant odour of the previous evening had been smothered by the smell of disinfectant. Neither could he hear the tinkling little bell. There was nothing else for it. He would have to make do with the room as it was.

Just the same, surveying the room more closely, he noted, in the corner, a cast-iron stove engraved with a representation of Abraham sacrificing Isaac. The scene was blasphemous, for it showed blood dripping down Abraham's arms, as if the patriarch had actually killed his son, while, in the biblical account, God had stayed Abraham's hand. The stove, he thought, would have been lit to aid decomposition of the corpses when the place had been a *leichenhauser.* The stench of putrefaction, he thought, must have been overwhelming. The thought of such things being too much for him, he decided to go down to the bar to see the landlord, finding him serving drinks.

'Mr Speigel,' he began ,'I've just heard the most extraordinary story from the proprietor of the Thuringia Inn. He said your hotel, and my room in particular, had once been part of a *leichenhauser*, a waiting mortuary. You never mentioned this to me when I booked in!'

Mr Spiegel looked guilty and broke off from serving his customer. 'But why would I, sir? It has been an inn for a long time now. And the girl has changed your mattress. I've had the room cleaned. You should have a good night's rest. The place is full tonight, but if you have another uncomfortable night, I'll change your room and refund you the overnight accommodation charge. That's fair, isn't it?

Recognising it would be churlish to refuse, he decided to make do with the room for one more night, though he wasn't terribly happy about his decision.

After downing several large brandies, he reluctantly returned to his room and got into bed. He could not put out the light out straight away, for the hairs on the back of his neck hadn't quite subsided. He took out, and began to read, his *Guidebook to Weimar.* All the while, he could not help imagining the naked corpses lying on the vacant beds around him, as would have been the case when it had been a *leichenhauser.* An hour later, succumbing to the fatigue of the day, his book toppled onto the floor, Mr Tulip falling asleep.

Perhaps, only two hours afterwards, he woke with the definite sensation that someone else was in the room. He looked around but saw nothing. Once more he heard the tinkling bell, had the irresistible desire to sneeze, smelt the sickening odour. But in the next instant he heard a soft thud, like the sound of a cat falling, plump, onto the floor. It was followed by a shuffling noise coming from the corner of the room furthest from his bed. If it was a cat, where had the cat come from? He had seen no cat in the hotel! His eyes strained into the darkness. Then he saw, next to the wardrobe and the internal door, a shadow; not the shadow of the wardrobe only, that was clear enough, but a vague and shapeless shadow that darkened the dull brown wall adjacent to it. Next he heard the sound of a wheezing breathing, as if of an asthmatic elderly patient who, he remembered, had passed by his hospital bed one night. With a dreadful reluctance he raised himself up on his elbows and allowed his eyes to turn towards the source of the sound. He saw a hooded thing, hunched over, arms extended, shuffling from bed to bed, examining each in turn. Then, after each unsatisfactory examination, it straightened up and screeched: '*That's not my bed!!*' As it came closer to his own bed. Mr Tulip wanted to scream, but found he could not. He wanted to leap out of bed and make a dash for the door, except he knew the door was securely locked, and the door key lay on the dresser. Did he dare try and run past it towards the internal door? No! It might intercept him! In a horrid perplexity he drew the sheet up over his face and began to recite the Lord's Prayer. But he had barely begun, when he felt the pressure of the creature's bony fingers running along the top of his eiderdown. Peeking out from behind the cover, he saw a deformed skull, with scraps of flesh still clinging to it; in short, he saw a skeleton, its grinning jaw hanging open, and felt its putrid breath. Its black empty eye-sockets now stared into his own. It drew back his covers, and he felt its horrible skull on his chest, the nasal aperture vigorously sniffing his flesh. Then it stood up, and suddenly screeched, '*You're in my bed!!*'

Mr Tulip could stand it no more. He confessed, afterwards, that he did not know what happened next, except that he found himself later in the night shivering on top of his mattress. His first grateful thought was, *I'm still alive!* His next was, *Where had it gone!* Without further ado, he rushed to the internal door, unlocked it and, still in his pyjamas, ran into the lounge where a grateful lamp still burned. He was found the following morning by the maid, quaking and as white as his bedsheet.

Refusing Mr Speigel's offer of a further free night's accommodation, he paid his bill and began his journey back to Blackstone Hall School, only stopping overnight in Calais out of necessity. Thankfully soon, he was back in England, but was distressed to see something grinning at him from behind a tree as he went along the school drive. Surely, he had left the horrors of the Thuringia Inn behind him? Minutes later, in blessed relief, he was in his familiar apartment. He felt safe at last! Though his nerves still jangled.

* * *

Unfortunately, not long after resuming his teaching duties, unable to sleep peacefully, he paged the matron of the school to call the doctor who, duly attended the distressed Mr Tulip. He diagnosed that the schoolmaster was suffering from a delirium, from which the person telling me the story said he never recovered. Indeed, Mr Tulip's last reported words to the doctor were, 'There's something in my bed!!'

## *Author's Note*

*The bodies in leichenhausers were laid out on wooden beds with bells tied to their toes, as an aid to detecting movement. In addition, the attendant would periodically tickle the nose of a corpse with a feather to check if the individual was dead. If the occupant sneezed, or if a tinkling bell was heard, the attendant knew the supposed corpse was a living person. The smell of putrefaction in these leichenhausers must have been appalling, with all the decaying corpses lying together in one room. Unfortunately, the attendant on watch was not permitted to leave his station, for fear of missing the tell-tale signs of life. For such a person, it was, literally, a life spent inside the House of the Dead. Many leichenhausers were built, not only in Weimar, but right across Germany, and in other continental countries. Some leichenhausers were also established in England. Even now, people fear being buried alive.*

# A Disappearance

I am not at all inclined to believe that prominent people disappear into thin air,. So I read the first letter from A.F. below with some scepticism (he only gives his initials). The same revealed that a northern-circuit judge, of some distinction, had suddenly vanished. It was sent to me, as someone interested in unusual tales, and it is published here for this reason. The author was the judge's nephew, writing to a friend. In my view the story is a very strange one, though I leave it to the reader to make up his own mind if he considers it to be so. The letters are clear and distinct. As they are better story tellers than my own hand, I leave it to them to convey the meaning of the narrative. The first letter is written by A.F. from Farleton Hall.

## I

## Farlton Hall, July 2nd 1838

It is with great regret that I will be unable to join yourself and

Lady Camilla for our tennis match this summer as we will be detained at Swanage. It seems Uncle Miles, having procured himself a hostelry (the Royal Oak) in that town, set off from there one morning and has not been seen or heard of since. As I write, there is no further information as to his whereabouts or about what might have happened to him. The missing persons' report (as read to me by Sergeant Phillips) simply states that Sir Miles left the Royal Oak at 2:30pm on the afternoon of June 24th, giving no-one reason to believe that he would not be returning to his table at 8:00pm for dinner at his usual time. If he planned to meet someone, he gave no indication of it. I have ascertained that, since his arrival on the 27th, he is reported to have spent most of his days atop the cliffs, or else along the shoreline, just as any normal tourist would have done. Indeed, it is frustrating that I am no wiser now than when I first received the news of his disappearance. Alas, I can hear the sound of the coach, so I will hand this letter to the clerk, for posting, hoping to arrive at Swanage sometime tomorrow. With cordial greetings to you all, your affectionate friend,

A.F.

## II

## Royal Oak, July 4th 1838

My Dear Alan,

Having arrived here two days ago, I am now extremely concerned for Uncle Miles. He has completely vanished and, I fear, we may not see him alive again. I say this because most of the things in his room are as he left them. There is no suggestion he had some business elsewhere which he kept to himself, though this cannot be ruled out. Furthermore, he has no friends in the vicinity on whom he might have called. None of his toiletries or other personal effects are missing, and even his favourite gold watch, given to him by Aunt Beatrice, is on his bedside table. He would certainly have taken this with him if he intended a permanent departure.

I am now in the process of reprimanding myself for not having spoken to Aunt Beatrice when I last saw her, concerning Uncle Miles's plans for his vacation. The stress of all this, incidentally, has resulted in Dr Tanner, her physician, advising her to take complete bed rest in case her heart condition worsens. A further disadvantage is that their only son, Harold, is away in Africa and cannot be easily contacted – although a letter has been despatched to him with the utmost urgency to his last address in Tanganyika, requesting his immediate return and detailing the circumstances. So, at the moment, it has fallen to me to take charge of things here.

Incidentally, according to an earlier conversation, Dr Tanner recently examined Sir Miles and found him neither halt nor lame, nor suffering from any malady of the mind. In addition, prior to departure, he was continuing in his charitable works in the district, including proffering legal advice to the younger barristers. These actions are not, you will agree, the mark of someone contemplating either professional or personal abdication. Indeed, to those who know him, the idea of such a notion is preposterous, including to Aunt Beatrice and, I must say to his closest legal peers and associates. But, please excuse me, I now put down my pen. I have a visitor in the person of Mr Strickland, a bear of a man, the innkeeper of the Royal Oak, who wishes to speak to me.

A.F.

## *Early evening*

Mr Strickland came to see me under the auspices of seeing if I had everything I wished. In reality, he wanted to impart some knowledge to me which he had withheld from the Metropolitan detectives, now they have finished their enquiries. I have been wondering, ever since, if this has left him open to the charge of obstruction of justice. Anyhow, the following is how the conversation began:

'Begging your pardon, sir,' he said, 'but I 'ave it on my mind to tell you something what I didn't tell the detectives. You must be the judge, sir, if you think there is any profit in it.'

Thereupon, he made an impassioned declaration that Miles, after a drink or two in the bar, had confided in him that, although on vacation, he was pursuing an enquiry about an escaped felon whom he had sentenced to prison years previously for grievous assault, but who had escaped.

'He told me, sir, if he could enjoy his vacation and, at the same time, apprehend the fellow – who he thought was possibly one of those gypsy people that travel with the fairs – he would consider his time well spent on both accounts. I did not tell the detectives anything of this, sir, for I 'ave 'ad troubles with the law in the past. Not anything for you to worry about, sir,' he quickly added, 'but I don't like to bring myself to their attention for fear they find some fault with my business and start checking my measures as, begging your pardon sir, they are inclined to do. You see, sir, I 'ave 'ad enough troubles lately, with the passing of my dear Bertha – God rest her soul – as good a wife as any man will find anywhere, and no suitable replacement in sight. So you see how it is, sir, why I didn't speak out to them detectives, and why I now come to be telling you of this. Only, I beg you sir, to keep it in your confidence and act on it as you might think fit. That is all I wish, sir.' And with that he was called away to the kitchen.

I must say, he looked mightily relieved by his confession, and later continued to check my understanding of his predicament, though I assured him I understood why he had not confided in the detectives and why, in the circumstances, I wouldn't fault his restraint. But in the early hours of the morning, it will occur to him that I *do* have my reservations, and I expect further excuses and protestations from him over the next couple of days, for a guilty conscience is not so easily assuaged.

Tomorrow I am going on a search of the cliffs and dunes, even though the police say their search has been exhaustive. I will write again afterwards, and send this letter by the late coach.

A.F.

## III

## Royal Oak, July 5$^{th}$ 1838

My Dear Alan,

As expected, my host at the Royal Oak seemed uneasy in his mind this morning. He addressed his servants over-loudly, particularly Molly, telling her he would serve me himself under the disguise of offering me more tea. I knew what was coming, and he again began to recount his reasons for keeping information from the detectives. They, incidentally, have returned to London complaining the trail had gone cold. I again tried to reassure Strickland that I attached no blame to his reticence, though I must confess to you that I thought he should have been more forthright with them, despite his reservations.

Probably in an effort to make amends, he accompanied us on our search of the cliffs, in which he was anything but helpful, suggesting we search here, now there, employing such phrases as, 'Perhaps he went down that gully there, sir?' or 'He might have gone further along the tops than we suppose, sir,' which possibilities, of course had already occurred to us. We were more than glad when he announced he could neglect his business no longer and would await our return at the inn, 'in hopeful expectation', as he puts it. Though, when we returned to the inn, we had no further news to report. Nevertheless, our landlord continues *in hopeful expectation.* He has taken to interrogating each new customer upon arrival, somehow convinced of the inevitability that someone will know of Miles's whereabouts. I think he is eaten up with guilt over Miles's death. The man really is a hopeless case.

But I have been diverted from my view of him, by a man called Sykes, an agricultural merchant from the West Country, who described a gay fair he had attended, and due to come to this part of the country. He recommended it for light relief, having been indiscreetly informed by Strickland of my situation. He particularly recommended the carousel ride which, at the time he saw it, boasted a large menagerie mounted on its rotating platform, saying it was 'the most splendid he had ever seen' and the finest outside Italy, which, he said, had the finest carousels in the whole world!

Not long afterwards, I retired to my room and fell quickly asleep on the couch. I began to have a vivid dream, as vivid as any I can remember. In it, I climbed aboard a colourful fairground carousel, similar to the one Sykes had described, which immediately set off – though there were spare places and other people were queuing. Shortly afterwards it began to increase in speed. At first, the ride was mildly pleasant, entertaining even, until someone pulled a lever. The music swelled to a crescendo and it began to rotate with increasing speed, so much so that I was forced to press my knees against the stallion I was riding. The velocity had suddenly become terrifying as I clung on to its mane for dear life. Faster and faster it rotated, until all around me became dark beyond the edge of the carousel. No longer could I see the cheerful faces and brightly lit stalls that I'd observed when I mounted. Though I had no objective means of estimating the speed at which I was travelling, it was obviously recklessly fast, for I was forced to lean inwards towards the carousel station, to counteract the centrifugal force of the spinning platform. The oddest thing was, that I felt as if I was travelling in a vacuum, for I could feel no pressure of wind upon my face. To my horror, my fellow riders seemed to be in the throes of wild exhilaration, having been completely spared the necessity of clinging onto their mounts, while I was in a state of acute anxiety.

Next, I saw my fellow riders had switched their mounts. Instead of flying horses, they were riding pigs, zebras – even a tiger. Others were mounted on mythological creatures, such as dragons, sea monsters, onocentaurs, unicorns and the like. I had just made this observation when I saw their mounts had broken free from their poles, running amok everywhere with their riders. What little illumination there now was, indicated that they had not the slightest concern for the chaos until, to their horror, the tiger, initially playful and carneying, resumed its predatory nature and started attacking the pig, which, by now, had lost its rider and was careering wildly about. Terrified for my own safety, I was forced to keep an ever-firmer hold of my mount for fear of spinning off into the darkness and joining them.

In the next instant, all semblance of it being a *carousella* vanished. The mythological creatures and their riders were still there – it is true – but they had lost all sense of propriety. The tiger, having despatched the pig, fixed upon myself as its next victim and, in no time, I felt its hot breath on my neck as it mounted the zebra, which was galloping alongside me. Suddenly, it braced itself on its back legs, preparing to pounce. Imagine my relief when, at that precise moment, I heard a long trumpet call which roused me from my slumbers, followed by several more blasts coming from the dunes. I promptly awoke, jumped off the couch and ran to the window, viewing the bright lights of a fair beyond. It seemed the exact same fair described by Mr Sykes. I'm afraid, I did not greet the sight with much enthusiasm, considering what had happened in my dream. Shortly afterwards, I went down to the half-empty bar, and downed a double brandy and soda. Thus fortified, I retired to my bed hoping there would be no repetition of the dream. Just the same, because of Sykes's recommendation, I determined to visit the fair the following evening.

A.F.

## IV

## Royal Oak, July 7th 1838

My Dear Alan,

It falls to me, now, to convey the desperately sad news that Uncle Miles *is* dead, though it is little short of extraordinary how he came to be found. The information below describes what transpired.

The following evening, after dinner, Strickland, who was preparing supper for some late guests, alerted by a creak of a floorboard on the stairs, took it upon himself to come out of the kitchen and investigate.

'Pardon me, sir,' he said, catching me on the bottom step, 'but I was only wondering where you was going this evening. I mean, sir, I would not wish to add to the recent calamity as we have had with your uncle, seeing that the perpetrator is likely still at large and might be anywhere hereabouts. Far be it from me, sir, to pry into anyone else's affairs, that is their business, but I still torture myself over what happened to Sir Miles and it would be more than I could stand if anything like it was to be repeated.'

Thus, I was obliged to advise him of my intended destination; namely, that I was off to the fair, promising him that I would take every care. That I only wanted to see the handsome carousel described by Mr Sykes, while the opportunity presented itself. I could not doubt his sincerity, however, for he watched me over the crest of the first dune as I made towards the music and bright lights of the fair. Quite frankly, I thought his imagination had got the better of him, though, of course, I refrained from saying so.

I must say, it was a strange thing to be walking across the hinterland in near darkness when, a short distance away, a vibrant performance was in full swing, though one in which, as yet, I had played no part. As I approached, I could see a coconut shy, rifle range and an illuminated sign inviting me to see 'THE STRANGE CREATURE FROM AFRICA'. I could see the brightly lit carousel, exactly like the one in my dreams and as described by Sykes, and I found myself drawn irresistibly towards it.

At first, I was content to watch the carousel orbit the control station, watching keenly as the riders embarked and disembarked at the toll of the bell. Thankfully, there was nothing of the chaos of my dreams of the night before. But I speak too soon, for it was then that I observed a swarthy-faced individual in the control station. He was watching me with such intense hostility that I was quite taken aback. Either he had mistaken me for someone else of his acquaintance – perhaps someone who had slighted him – or he recognised me for who I was, the nephew of Uncle Miles, and regarded me as a threat. I considered the latter case slightly more credible, given the conversation with Strickland about Miles pursuing a fellow from the gypsy community. I estimated he must have been watching me for some time. I was about to approach the carousel station to address him, when he suddenly handed over the controls to an assistant and, as sure-footed as a mountain goat, danced across the rotating platform and disappeared into the darkness. Though not before checking that I was following him – which I was – and we were both soon lost in the darkness of the coast, stumbling blindly along towards the sea and the cliffs, the bright lights and sounds of the carousel fading behind us.

Reaching a position on the cliffs where, I fancied, he might have climbed down, I began a precarious descent and, after about ten minutes, I found myself on a narrowing ledge some sixty feet above the rocky beach, the sound of waves crashing below me. Just as I was about to return, thinking I had mistaken his intentions, I observed an opening in the cliff behind me, a sort of small cave. Groping my way into its black interior, two strong arms immediately grabbed me by the throat, and forced me out onto the ledge. It could be for no other reason than to send me crashing down onto the rocks below. I knew, instinctively, it was the gypsy, and I also knew, if I couldn't resist him, my fate was sealed. Though I summoned up all my strength, I began to lose ground. As we exited the cave, a sudden shaft of moonlight came out from behind the clouds and I read the look of malevolent hatred in his eyes which, as I neared the edge, changed to one of triumph. I redoubled my efforts, but I was unable to prevail against him. Soon I would be crashing down onto the rocks below.

And that, dear Alan, is exactly what would have happened, had not Strickland suddenly appeared out of the gloom and smashed a stone down onto the gypsy's skull, causing him to collapse and topple soundlessly over the edge onto the rocks below. Badly winded, I sank to my knees, imagining that the gypsy's fate would have been mine a few faltering moments ago. Looking up, I thanked Providence. Looking up at Strickland, my gratitude knew no bounds.

'Are you alright, sir?' he asked.

I was too breathless to speak.

He continued casually. 'Like I said, sir, it wouldn't do to 'ave anything 'appen to another gentleman at my inn. I've my reputation to think of. He helped me to my feet. 'And now, sir, if you permit me, I'll escort you back there and no harm done to yourself, apart from a close shave with the Devil.'

I could hardly believe my luck. And I learnt later that he had been following me the whole time. After I had recovered my senses, I began to feel a pang of remorse that my opinion of Strickland hitherto, had been somewhat derogatory, and I thought to reward him in some way.

The following morning, at first light, the constables recovered the body (for the tide had not yet claimed him) and, after enquiries at the fair, he was identified as one John Swaggart, the same escaped felon tried by Uncle Miles and sent to prison for the manslaughter of a young woman a few years earlier. This, no doubt, was why Uncle Miles had pursued him down to the south coast. He never could tolerate any kind of violence against a woman. Furthermore, I could understand why he would not have wanted to tell Aunt Beatrice of his suspicions, for fear of worrying her. Unfortunately, it is also my sad duty to report that a further search of the cave revealed Uncle Miles's decomposing body in the recess. He had, according to the post-mortem, been strangled. Probably, he had followed Swaggart in the same way as I had done, but with no saviour in the personage of Mr Strickland to save him. The only consolation is that Swaggart will never again bother any member of the fair sex. To my mind, uncle Miles died a hero, upholding the law to the fullest extent. My host at the Royal Oak, Mr Strickland, promises to regale residents of his establishment with this story for years to come, dwelling, no doubt, on the central part he took in my rescue and the apprehension of the villain; though, I must say, it would be churlish to deny that he is entitled to some glory.

It only remains to say that I have written, of course, to Aunt Beatrice offering my condolences, advising her of Uncle Miles's death, stressing that he gave his life in pursuit of justice and honour., and that she should be proud of his actions. He had both done his duty according to the lights of his profession, and as a highly moral individual. I hope my remarks will provide her with some comfort. The funeral will be in three weeks' time, on July 29th, but, no doubt, word will soon circulate. I imagine it will be quite a gathering, given the large number of acquaintances and friends who will wish to attend.

But one thing still puzzles me, and I must ask you when we meet again, regarding the carousel, if you think my dream about it, and Sykes' recommendation to visit it, was simply a coincidence or that my attraction to it, and the subsequent sighting of Swaggart, and so on, poses a higher-order mystery?

With cordial greetings to you all, your affectionate friend,

A.F.

# A School Story

'Benton! Campbell! Roberts!' called out Miss St Clair, her fine clear voice soaring up into the rafters; the bright, eager faces of the mainly infant schoolchildren fixed upon her. It was her first day at Molton C of E School in Lincolnshire, tucked under the Wolds, next to the village church, surrounded by fields and woodland. Indeed, it was her first day ever of teaching ever. Time seemed to stand still as she stopped calling their names and her complexion turned rosey red. There had been no response from the children to their names being called. She scanned the cover and saw it was the Reverend Crannage's register for last year's class. How had it ended up on her desk? Had the caretaker mistakenly placed it there?

Outside, the strengthening January wind flung flurries of snow against the casements, leaving white deposits high up on the Victorian window ledges – windows too high for little children to see out of. It whitened the windows of the nearby Church. At the back of the classroom, a large black kettle chirped quietly on the range, ready to fill the mugs of cocoa for the children at break time. While they waited, the children drew pictures on their slates, while Miss St Clair found and proudly called the correct register. She put the Rev Crannage's register back in her desk drawer, puzzling as to its appearance.

The kettle began to boil, and the children went and sat on the benches, near the fire. The monitors poured the hot water into mugs of cocoa, adding milk and sugar according to taste. The children drank eagerly. A hot drink on a cold morning was particularly welcome for, despite the roaring fire, there was still a definite chill in the rural classroom. Fifteen minutes afterwards, the monitors called time and the mugs were collected and washed. The chatter subsided. The children resumed their seats. Her class, partly distracted by the falling snow, seemed disinclined to work, so she read them the story of the Three Little Pigs. The eyes of the children widened excitedly as the wolf came close to the pigs' house. There was near pandemonium when the beast fell down the chimney into the pot!

As it was still snowing at lunch time, Miss St Clair kept the children indoors, allowing them to play games. The din was deafening, and she was glad when the lunch period ended and order was restored. She felt pleased that the school day was going reasonably well.

However, things were about to change. Shortly after the children opened their reading books, an unusually large raven with blue-purple iridescent plumage, alighted high up on a windowsill and began striking the glass with its beak, as if demanding admission. She tried to shoo it away with a duster tied to the top of the window pole, yet it continued its aggressive *tap*, *tap*, *tap*, much to the delight of the children and Miss St Clair's annoyance.

The schoolmistress continued with her lessons as best she could, disrupted by the noisy bird until, at fifteen minutes past three, her first school day came to an end and the children departed to go to their homes. It was still snowing heavily, all around was a white wasteland, and some of them lived several miles away. She knew that one little boy, and his sister, had to walk three miles to Bowfield Farm. Eventually, the last snowball fights subsided in the playground until, finally, the grounds were deserted. Miss St Clair went up to her residential rooms, grateful that the caretaker had lit the fire for her. While her dinner of pork was cooking, she read Charles Kingsley's *The Water Babies*, and the fairy tale, *Little Red Riding Hood*, intending to read one or the other to the class the following day. *At least you've got through your first day!* she congratulated herself, concerned she could still hear the raven tapping on the classroom window below. What an odd bird it was, she thought, as she ate her dinner of pork and potatoes. She must get rid of it. As she climbed into bed that first night in residence at Molton School, her mind returned to the interview with the School board that autumn. She could still hear the squire's voice, cautioning:

'You may hear rumours, Miss St Clair, about our old school house being haunted, but these rumours only have to do with the... er, the age of the building, and not to do with any other, goings-on.' He looked at the doctor and rector for support, who docilely nodded their agreement. 'While it is true, our caretaker, Mr Whatley, has never himself resided in the building overnight, as you will be required to do, he has on countless occasions been in the school early of a darkened morning or evening, and he tells me he has never heard or seen anything, how shall I put it… unusual. Which is to say, there is absolutely no need for you to listen to the wagging tongues in the village, about ghosts and the like – unless you want to scare yourself to death – as did, your predecessor, Miss Catkins, who ran out of the school in the middle of the night, last summer, the result of listening to old wives' tales. *Wasn't that so gentlemen?* His fellow interviewers again nodded their agreement. 'You are not, I trust, Miss St Clair, of a nervous disposition, like your predecessor?'

In all honesty, Miss St Clair thought not, and said so. 'I don't believe in ghosts, sir, for it's not part of my Christian upbringing. I was always taught not to discuss such things. My father and mother are devout Anglicans, and I've followed in their footsteps.'

'Quite right! Quite right! Miss St Clair,' said the rector, 'that's exactly the attitude I would have wished to hear in an upright Christian woman.' He smiled at the doctor and the squire. There was some mumbling between them and, a short time afterwards, Miss St Clair was offered the post of Assistant Schoolmistress in the small Lincolnshire village of Molton. Thrilled at her appointment, she stepped out of the village's Moot Hall, where the interviews had taken place, only to have her bubble pricked by an old woman who poked her with her walking stick, and said, 'Be gone from the school before the light fades, or you'll meet a sour-faced ghost.' And, with that, she began her journey home.

Though Miss St Clair had paid little attention to the remark at the time, believing the woman to be an eccentric, now, as it grew dark, and she could hear several creaks and groans coming from the classroom below, the old woman's unwelcome words came back to her. Furthermore, Whatley, the caretaker, had said that Miss Catkins had persisted with her duties, even though she had always felt nervous about being in the building after dark; until, one terrible night, she had run screaming out of the school in the early hours, ending up in a mental asylum in Lincoln. Thereafter, the poor woman had returned to her home in Scotland and had resigned her post. The caretaker had also said that Miss Catkins had sometimes complained of 'noises' in the school, particularly during the hours of darkness, *and the sounds of comings and goings in the classroom below.* She had asked him if he had ever come into the building at night, moving the teacher's chair and the children's benches, and so on, though he said he had not.

Now, as she listened, she thought she *could* actually hear someone moving about in the classroom below. It was as if the teacher's chair was being continually drawn up and moved back, and she thought she could hear the sound of the children's benches being moved. *How odd?* she thought. Unlocking her apartment door, descending the small staircase to the corridor, she called out Whatley's name, but received no answer. Slowly, reluctantly, she crept along the corridor towards the classroom from which the bangings noises were emanating. When the noises stopped abruptly, as she reached the door, her heart jumped into her throat. It was as if someone had been walking from one bench to another, throwing down the children's slates, rearranging the benches. A moment later, as she listened outside of the door, there came the screech of chalk on the blackboard. *Who was writing a message at this time of night!? Was the caretaker writing a message for her to find it in the morning?* She knew if she opened the door, she would come face to face with whatever was within. In a horrid perplexity, she found she could not continue, and raced back along the corridor, dashing up the stairs to her apartment. She slammed and locked the door behind her, leaning breathless with her back upon the door knob. *But, wait a minute! Was the knob rotating? Was someone trying to enter her apartment?* She fled to her bed in the corner of the room, cowering, staring horrified at the door. She could not tell if it was her imagination turning the knob, or it was really turning? After a long while, her pulse slowed, and she regained some sort of composure. Deciding that she needed some fresh air, she tiptoed to the window and opened it, promptly closing it again after a black feathered wing brushed against her arm. Was it the raven?

It was a very long time before Miss St Clair could get herself into bed, and she could not remember when she had managed to fall asleep. The morning found her propped up on two pillows, recalling a nightmare in which she was chased by a black-cloaked murderer around an old building. The murderer had accused her of stealing an exercise book from the school! Despite vehemently protesting her innocence, his pursuit continued until she noticed, to her horror, a book under her arm, justifying the murderer's attempt to kill her! In desperation, she threw the book over her shoulder, hoping the pursuer would stop to pick it up, but he only quickened his pace after her. With extraordinary relief, she awoke and heard someone moving about below. She descended the stairs.

'That's funny,' said Whatley, meeting her in the corridor, 'there's footprints in the snow leading from the school door, to the lane. It looks as if someone left the building in the middle of the night, judging from how they're pointing. Did you have a visitor, Miss?'

She stared in astonishment at the two sets of footprints. One made by the caretaker in his approach to the building, the other leading away from it. 'Look,' he said, going into the classroom, 'there's melted snow in here, too, and in the corridor!' Miss St Clair saw there was a substantial pool of water on the floor of the classroom. Whatley looked up. 'See up there, there's a small pane of glass broken high up in the window. I've not seen anything like that before, Miss, not even when the Reverend Crannage was here! Are you sure you didn't have a visitor last night, miss?'

Miss St Clair thought quickly, realising that ghostly noises didn't make footprints. But how could she explain them without his thinking that she was just another weak-minded Miss Catkins, frightened of bumps and bangs in the night? It would invite ridicule and raise suspicions about her mental state, apart from the fact that the school board didn't permit her to have visitors after nightfall.

'Of course not,' she replied, keeping the deception out of her voice, 'I can't think of how it happened.'

Whatley shook his head and went outside to examine the exterior of the building, returning with a puzzled look on his face.

'I just don't understand how this glass came to be broken, Miss. There aren't no footprints around that side of the building. It's almost as if someone flew up to the window and broke it!

Miss St Clair seized her opportunity.

'Well,' she volunteered, remembering the bird, 'there was a large raven striking with its beak against the pane all day yesterday, disturbing our lessons. In fact, it was still there when I left the classroom and went up to my apartment last night. I imagine *it* broke the glass!'

Whatley looked sceptical.

'Well, I don't know about that, Miss, but I'll have to report it to the School Board. The glazier will have to come and the repair will cost money. For now, I'll get my ladder and block up the hole with a bit of paper or cardboard. That's the best I can do.' He turned to look sympathetically at the tired Miss St Clair. 'By the way, Miss,' he said, 'you look pale and rather shaken. Perhaps the strain of starting your new job. Would you like me to make you a cup of tea?'

Miss St Clair could have kissed him, and subsequently took the tea up to her room, trying to recover her composure before the children arrived. How long would she be able to remain at the school if the frightening experience of the previous evening was repeated? Was she not surprised that Miss Catkins had fled the building in the middle of the night, if what had happened to her had also happened to her predecessor. Yet what could she do? She could not give up her post on the basis of one night's disturbances. There must, she thought, be some simple explanation for what had happened, and earnestly hoped there would not be a repeat of the events.

Fortified by the tea, she went outside and rang the handbell. The children lined up and, upon her command, filed into the classroom. She sat down. Oddly, the Rev Crannage's register was once again on her desk. A tear ran down her cheek in frustration. Was today to be a repeat of yesterday? To make matters worse, the raven returned mid-morning and was again striking with its beak against the windowpane. It continued its rumbustious behaviour throughout the day. Oddly, it would sometimes pause and look directly at her, as if it believed there was some common bond between them. It looked, for all the world like the Reverend Crannage, whose picture hung at the rear of the classroom, with its tail feathers looking exactly like his black cloak stretched out behind him. They both had the same bright, twinkling, eyes.

After the children had gone home, Miss St Clair did her best to maintain her evening routine, and promptly, at ten o'clock, she completed her toilet and went to bed, dreaming that the register she had called that morning had gone missing again, and that the raven high up on the windowsill was holding it in its beak. It flew down onto the teacher's chair, metamorphosing into the sour-faced Reverend Crannage, then proceeded to call out the children's names. Her pupils now clamoured, not for cocoa, but for mugs of birdseed which the raven duly served from a barrel next to the teacher's desk. She pointlessly remonstrated with him, saying that this was *her* class. But the clergyman only shouted, 'I'm the teacher here!' The children screeched their agreement, having now turned into little birds.

Whether it was the frustration of the dream, or the banging noises coming from the classroom below, at two o'clock Miss St Clair once more heard the teacher's chair being drawn up and pulled back, the sound of benches being moved. Did she have the courage to investigate? She must! How else could she continue her teaching at the school? She put on her dressing gown, and with a terrible reluctance, descended the stairs, creeping barefoot along the corridor to the classroom door. As before, the moment she reached the door the noises ceased. Again there followed a loud screech of chalk on the blackboard, only this time it was followed by the sound of footsteps coming closer to where she stood. Whatever it was, would soon come into view. She could not wait. She must see what it was! With every ounce of courage she possessed, she pushed through the door and walked into the classroom.

What happened next was not known. The following morning the caretaker found Miss St Clair lying face up, dead, on the classroom floor. Next to her was the bloodied corpse of a raven and, in its beak, it held a piece of chalk. Shocked and traumatised, the caretaker called the police.

'Looks like it's pecked out her eyes,' said the doctor, examining the empty eye sockets. 'And look here! See the claw marks on her cheeks! It must have perched there on her face in order to gain purchase. Look at the size of the raven's beak, its ruffled neck feathers! What a huge bird! I didn't know they were capable of such vicious attacks.'

'I must say,' said the police inspector, 'I've never known one to enter a building and attack someone like this before, though I know they can attack humans outdoors near their nests. But surely those marks weren't the cause of death?'

The doctor rubbed his chin. 'By the expression on her face, I'd say she died of fright… and probably in the early hours of the morning. I've seen soldiers who died of fright with a similar expression. My medical certificate will say the cause death was cardiac arrest. We don't want to make fools of ourselves.'

They left the school and, as Miss St Clair had no living relatives, the poor woman was buried at the Parish's expense in the local churchyard.

When Miss Simmons arrived to take Miss St Clair's place

for the duration of the term, she was puzzled why the Reverend Crannage's register kept appearing on her desk, and why the current register kept disappearing into her desk drawer. As she went to bed in the school apartment that first night, she was disturbed by noises emanating from the classroom below, and it was not long before she went to investigate.

# The Blood of the Lamb

Lord Asconby, the ailing owner of Doll Hall, was a learned and inquisitive man, who took a keen interest in his own mortality. His two-hundred-acre parkland estate, in the county of Gloucestershire, was pleasantly bisected by a tributary of the River Avon, forming a pleasant meadow on which sheep, cows and the inevitable horses, grazed. Fallow deer wandered freely throughout the park, providing Lord Asconby with venison. A more pleasant location was difficult to imagine and, I dare say, his joy would have been complete were it not for his circulatory ailments.

Architecturally, the attractive hall had sympathies with both the Queen Anne and the Gothic, and the combination was overwhelmingly uplifting. From the large leaded, west-facing, windows there were pleasant views over a green vale towards misty hills. The wooded grounds were populated with oak, pine and birch, which Lord Asconby had planted to screen the hall from prying eyes; for, despite the charming vista, his lordship was a secretive man with a nose perpetually in books, particularly, though not surprisingly, those dealing with human physiology. A stone-pillared porch had been added in about 1780, which further charmed the building. A Palladian folly could be seen to the west, and it was behind this that the sun was now setting, illuminating the two wings of Doll Hall which curved outwards from the main body of the house, rather like a pair of scorpion's pincers ready to intercept prey. It was on this evening that Dr Hinchcliffe dismounted from his horse and ran up the steps to the main door in expectation of a profitable visit to the ailing peer.

The doctor thumped the knocker as the last rays of the sun winked at him from behind the folly, and the clock in the tower struck six in the afternoon, the agreed hour of his appointment with Lord Asconby. As the doctor had ridden towards the hall, he had been sharpening his wits, for it was his intention to persuade the wealthy gentleman to submit to the risky procedure of a blood transfusion, aimed at restoring the peer's failing circulatory system. A pioneering and unsafe medical procedure at the time, his plan was to perform the procedure on his elderly patient in return for a substantial sum of money. Indeed, the doctor had already expended significant sums on preliminary experiments, involving transfusions between pairs of rabbits and lambs, as pioneered by doctors Harvey and Blundell. Unfortunately in transfusing the blood of donor creatures into their ailing companions, there had been spectacular failures, for the doctor had confused the reflexive movement in the limbs of such creatures with those of vital life, as for example, when the limbs of a dog twitch asleep by a fire. Undaunted, he had supplemented these efforts with modest amounts of electrical stimulation. Even so, he was still only able to achieve partial resurrection. But, he reasoned, these creatures did not have the vitality of human life; that is, humans' greater desire to live which, he hoped, would make up the difference. He was bolstered in this view in reading that

Pope Innocent VIII had been given the blood of three ten-year-old boys to drink. Unfortunately, the boys subsequently died with no substantial benefit to the prelate, and it had not occurred to him that the story was probably a Jewish blood libel.

The door to the hall swung open and the medical man was shown into Lord Asconby's library. Inside, he quickly explained his proposal, not wishing to linger over the details for fear of betraying his lack of confidence and ignorance in the procedure. As may be imagined, Lord Asconby was no fool, and was reluctant to agree to the unproven treatment but, as his health was reaching a critical point, he let himself be persuaded. For it is the case, that even a drowning man will clutch at straws.

'There is just one thing,' the doctor continued, having obtained his agreement, 'there is a need to secure the services of a willing human donor who can be close at hand at the vital moment. We must have a suitable reservoir of blood, we cannot go searching for one at the last minute!'

'Go on,' said the peer.

'The donor will have to be as large as a stout boy, of good health and physique. Fresh blood will immediately be required when your heart begins to fail, and we need to procure a convenient and ready supply of the oxygenating fluid well in advance.'

'So you must find me one,' urged Lord Asconby, 'if that is what is required.'

Dr Hinchcliffe, as may be imagined, had already thought of the answer, though he pretended otherwise.

'In my view, the perfect donor would need to be available both night and day, such as a boy about whom no awkward questions might be asked, in the event of a medical accident. I can't absolutely guarantee the life of the donor will be preserved. An orphan boy, without living relatives would be ideal. As a matter of fact,' he confided, 'I've already seen a chubby boy called Tom, of almost ten years of age, a resident of the local workhouse. I'm sure the lad could be procured without too many awkward questions being asked.'

'Very well, I'll leave it in your hands,' said the peer, and it was agreed that Dr Hinchcliffe would visit the workhouse the following day, where he was the chief physician. All being well, he would send Tom up to Doll Hall at the earliest opportunity, in order that preparations might be made for his lordship's transfusion.

The next day, the doctor lost no time in asking the workhouse superintendent to send Tom to him and, after a satisfactory medical examination, in which the doctor made sure they were out of earshot, he addressed the lad, directly:

'Poor Tom,' he began sympathetically. 'Poor Tom, you *have* fallen on hard times,' ruffling the boy's hair. 'But you know, dear boy, Providence may sometimes lift up a poor boy like yourself to a better station in life. It has been known to happen!' He smiled generously. 'Dear lad, I believe that this is the day you will consider that I, as Providence's servant, have come to give relief to your poor body, the one God blessed you with. Oh, dear Tom, only seize this opportunity now to raise yourself up and you'll find great opportunities lie ahead; for, Tom, Lord Asconby has told me that he has need of a boy such as yourself up at Doll Hall.' Tom nodded uncomprehendingly. 'No family living who might provide you with relief, dear Tom?' Tom shook his head. 'Oh dear, all alone in the world. Poor lad! No mother or father, brother or sister, or aunt or uncle?'

'No sir, none living.'

'Well, well, dear lad, we can focus on your welfare and yours alone. No need to tell the workhouse superintendent of your good fortune. We'll keep it as our little secret, shall we?' He pinched Tom's cheeks with false affection, smiling beneficently.

Tom nodded.

'Oh, but what a fine, sturdy, boy you are, Tom... I'm sure Lord Asconby will be glad when he sees how strong you are. Oh, the pleasures that await you up at Doll Hall! I can see you there now, my lad, partaking of the finest viands, and the sweetest of drinks. I take it that you like lemonade, fruit drinks, Tom?'

'Yes sir!'

'Well, I fancy you won't be able to stop eating and drinking, at the hall, Tom. But don't spoil your good fortune by letting others in on our secret. Don't tell a single soul. Not a word to anyone!'

'Yes, sir, I mean, no, sir.'

'Quite right. The hand of Providence must not be thwarted!'

'Yes, sir, I mean, no, sir.'

So it was, according to Dr Hinchcliffe's plan, a few days later arrangements were made for Tom to run away from the workhouse one night, while the other inmates and staff were sleeping. Dr Hinchcliffe lent the boy his own key to the workhouse back door, with the instruction to creep silently down and let himself out, and meet the doctor at the bottom of the lane.

'And don't leave the key in the lock, Tom, or you'll be back at the workhouse!' warned the doctor. 'Lord Asconby doesn't want a careless boy up at the hall!

'Yes, sir, I mean I won't!'

And so the arrangements were made.

In case the reader was wondering if Lord Asconby was a cruel man, who cared nothing for Tom's welfare, this must be resisted for, in other matters, he was a generous benefactor. It was simply that, like many wealthy and powerful men, he was reluctant to contemplate an early death. Neither had Dr Hinchcliffe taken the peer fully into his confidence regarding the likely effects of the transfusion on the boy; namely, that the boy was likely to die, for the untried practice of blood transfusion had largely been abandoned by the medical profession at that time. Furthermore, in the likelihood of an untoward medical event, concerning the boy, the doctor would seek to hide his errors under the high mortality rates prevailing at the time. Who would concern themselves with the death of a pauper, least of all a friendless orphan; even one that lived at Doll Hall? Just the same, the doctor sought to salve his conscience with the thought that the peer would at least give the lad a decent Christian burial, which was a better resting place than a pauper's grave.

'There you are, Tom!' said the doctor, handing the boy over to Mrs Grant, the housekeeper at Doll Hall. 'Feed him up well, Mrs Grant. Poor Tom has not had the nourishment he needs at the workhouse and, if he is to accomplish the tasks Lord Asconby has in mind for him, he will need to put on a lot more weight. Isn't that right, Tom?'

'Yes, sir!' said Tom, the thought of the vittles uppermost in his mind.

'Plenty of steak and kidney pies. Plenty of bread and butter, jam and cakes? That's what he needs Mrs Grant?'

'Yes, sir.' Tom's eyes seemed almost to bulge at the prospect of all the food.

'See to it, then, Mrs Grant, for I'm to charge you, on Lord Asconby's account, to give him as much food as he wants. He may already look like a chubby lad to you, but there's more room for nourishment yet, right, Tom?'

The doctor smiled kindly at the lad, again pinching his cheeks.

'I'll do your bidding, sir,' replied Mrs Grant, 'as my master has instructed,' and she went to the kitchen and opened a cupboard door. Tom ogled at the pie-filled shelves, and it was all he could do to stop himself reaching out for a freshly baked one, particularly the one with the tempting aroma of baked fruit.

'Good, good,' confirmed the doctor. 'I expect to see much more of you, Tom, when I call at the hall again. Ha, ha!'

Mrs Grant drew the boy towards her, smothering his face in her bosom, then kissing him on the forehead. 'I can assure you, you'll not go hungry at Doll Hall, my precious!'

From Tom's point of view, of course, Doll Hall was an infinitely more pleasant place than the workhouse and, as might be expected, he wolfed down increasing quantities of cakes, pastries, scones, pies and other vittles. Within a few weeks, he was almost twice the lad who had first come to the hall.

The only thing Tom objected to was the strange leather-covered couch on wheels, upon which he was made to sleep each night. Neither did he care for the room itself, surrounded as he was by glass bottles, rubber tubes, drip stands and all manner of other medical paraphernalia. Also, because it was leather, the blankets would keep slipping off his increasingly chubby legs. He disliked the strong smell of disinfectant and wondered why he could not sleep in a proper bed like the other servants, and why there was an exactly similar leather couch drawn up tight against his own, which always remaining unoccupied?

To this latter enquiry, Mrs Grant explained that Dr Hinchcliffe had wanted to keep it vacant in case his benefactor took ill during the night.

'For in that case, Tom, Lord Asconby will need your comforting presence, lying next to him. Doctors know best!'

Naively, Tom was satisfied with this explanation, for he could not complain about the food, or that he did not have the run of the estate, or about the many other kindnesses Lord Asconby showed him. And why should he *not* comfort his benefactor?

The arrangement continued. Inevitably, Lord Asconby took ill and was brought down and placed on the couch next to

Tom. Soon Tom felt a painful stab in his arm as the procedure commenced. As the transfusion progressed, Tom slipped into unconsciousness until, finally, he passed away. Alas, neither the infused blood nor the electrical stimulation administered to Lord Asconby could sustain his benefactor. The outcome was not surprising, for inevitably, the doctor had entirely failed to understand his patient's immunological reaction to the boy's blood, resulting in the release of free haemoglobin into Lord Asconby's circulation. Consequently Tom had given up his life for nothing. Unusually, Lord Asconby and Tom shared the same funeral eulogy, and Tom's body was buried in the family churchyard, next to his heir-less benefactor. Lord Asconby's death was recorded as 'cardiac arrest', and that of Tom's, 'circulatory failure'. As for Dr Hinchcliffe, it was apposite that he had been paid for his services in advance, for he was able, at last, to be able to repay his gambling debts. The rest of the money he squandered on travelling extensively abroad, where he indulged in unrestricted lasciviousness and debauchery; and, in the process, contracted a venereal disease.

A few months later, when he had run out of cash, Dr Hinchcliffe sought to replenish his funds by visiting the new owner of Doll Hall, who, as chance would have it, also experienced cardiac difficulties. The doctor intended to repeat the procedure he had performed for Lord Asconby; this time, hopefully, with better results. Perhaps the new owner would have a stronger constitution. Perhaps it was Lord Asconby's fault that he died during the transfusion. The peer had never been a suitable subject in the first place!

However, in pursuit of performing the same procedure for the new owner of Doll Hall, it is the case that, as the doctor galloped up the drive to Doll Hall, his horse caught a glimpse of a chubby, white-faced boy beneath the trees. It so frightened his animal that it threw its rider into the fountain, impaling the medical man on the central prong of Poseidon's Trident, from which gushed a torrent of water. Alas, the poor doctor died a few minutes later.

Mrs Grant, looking out of an upstairs window, witnessed the doctor's accidental death, and swore to the magistrate that, a few seconds before the horse reared up and threw the doctor into the fountain, she'd seen Tom's chubby ghost leap out in front of the horse, waving his outstretched arms. Her account was confirmed for a long time afterwards, by visitors to the hall who reported seeing the ghost of a chubby boy along the wooded borders of the hall's drive, matching Tom's description.

The image faded until, some few years later, it disappeared altogether. Oddly, though, after Tom's death, Mrs Grant noticed that an invisible someone was helping themselves to cakes and scones from the kitchen pantry; and, once or twice, she had followed the trail of crumbs to the medical room where Tom had slept.

'Oh, Tom!' she said, coming into the room on a further occasion, 'you are naughty!'

It must be considered, therefore, that perhaps, Tom had not left the hall after all!

# The Wine Cellar

Sir Charles Pomeroy's illness resisted all cures. The most powerful medications had no effect. Even the best psychiatrists found themselves helpless. Yet they had to do *something* to help Sir Pomeroy. After all, it was *his* money that had paid for Garland Mental Hospital to be built in the first place, the mental hospital in which he now resided.

Dr Crabb's idea was to return him to Chittington Manor, his ancestral home, hoping that the familiar surroundings would serve as a tonic. Dr Simons, on the other hand, cautioned against such a course of action on the grounds that it was not sound psychiatric practice and might lead to a regression in the patient. Nevertheless, at Dr Crabb's insistence (as the senior physician), Sir Charles was returned to Chittington Manor. Dr Simon's psychiatric notes, now in my possession, together with the diary Sir Pomeroy kept, describe what followed. They show how a fairly innocuous event can spiral into tragedy. I start with some medical notes by Dr Simmons.

* * *

Dr Crabb's plan to return Sir Pomeroy to Chittington Manor has caused a marked regression in the patient. He now exhibits heightened emotional ability, and attacked Nurse Johnson with whom he had previously enjoyed good relations, biting her severely on the hand and vehemently accusing her of being a co-conspirator of Dr Crabb. He now lashes out with his feet and fists, and it takes not one, but three strong nurses to subdue him. He has recently exhibited another derangement; namely, he will not put his foot down anywhere on the floor, in any part of the hospital, without someone first walking in front of him and planting *their* feet there first. Then, with a painful reluctance, he will follow in those footsteps – when he is inclined to follow at all. However, if he puts his foot down somewhere which he thinks the leading person has not put theirs, either actually or in his imagination, he becomes petrified on the spot. No amount of cajoling will move him. It is almost as if he has stepped on a landmine and fears, if he lifts his foot, an ordnance will detonate. Naturally, we keep him on the strongest sedatives, and we continue to hope that time itself will undermine his paranoia and improve his health. But I must say, he looks quite mad; his eyes dart wildly about, suspicious of everything, and he engages in episodes of sniggering and giggling, playing peek-a-boo behind his hands. On these occasions, his countenance switches between one of sombre normality to that of a deranged imbecile. He repeats this 'face covering' behaviour countless times a day and is becoming a parody of himself in the struggle between the apparently sane Sir Pomeroy and the latent madman.

Of course, no-one is insane all of the time and, I must say, for a psychotic Sir Charles did manage to keep a diary right up until the time of his admission to Garland. At times, he is extraordinarily lucid and circumscribed. The first entry gives a clue to his ensuing mental turmoil, believing that a person, called Harold was a usurper. The same Harold had entered his house claiming to be a long-lost relative and entitled to an equal share of his estate and, further proposing marriage to his daughter, Eleanor. The idea of either prospect was anathema to him. We can now read the first extract in his diary, dated the sixteenth of September, 1863. These notes are not in chronological order. The first entry gives a flavour of his troubles:

*Sir Charles Pomeroy's diary (dated 16.9.1863)*

All of life now seems a blessed relief now that Harold, the 'great pretender', has gone. With him, he has taken the threat to my eighteen-thousand-acre estate and the threat of marriage to my beautiful daughter. It all began when the bounder turned up one night at Chittington Manor, claiming to be a long-suffering victim of amnesia (from which handicap, he claimed, he had recently recovered), saying that he was the illegitimate child of a woman my father had known in St Lucia. Initially, I did the decent thing, granting him admission to Chittington, while I made enquiries about his supposed claim to the estate. As it happens, there does seem to be a garbled account in my father's diary about a Lucian woman who my father was fond of, though there was no mention of progeny. What has infuriated me more than the extravagant claims to my estate, is that he says he has fallen in love with, and proposes to marry, Eleanor, my treasured daughter. 'She has won my heart!' he proclaimed, shortly after meeting her. 'Baa! Humbug!' This assertion, I knew, had more to do with his establishing a claim over my estate than to any genuine love for that attractive creature. Needless to say, he received no encouragement from me on either account. Sadly, Eleanor can't see him for what he really is: a scoundrel and a fraud undoubtedly after her fortune. Remonstrating with her at length has produced no change in her attitude. I confess, I've never seen a woman so infatuated with a man! He continues to drone on about his right to a share of Chittington Manor. The following extract is a typical example:

'You must let me have half,' he said, referring to the estate, pacing up and down the room, hand on hip, tossing his head like a stallion. 'Half is all I ask, and then I shall leave you in peace!'

'Peace will never be mine while you are this side of the grave,' I retorted. 'As for marrying Eleanor, I forbid it. Forbid it now and forever. There will be no union.' But I might as well not have spoken. He left the room, slamming the door behind him, clearly impervious to reason.

*Sir Charles Pomeroy's diary (dated 15.7.1863)*

I am beginning to form a plan to rid myself of the detestable Harold. It occurs to me, if things take a legal turn for the worse, I might lose the greater part of my estate – for he is certainly an accomplished and convincing liar. Worse! I now find he may actually have some proof to back up his claim. Eleanor, of course, continues to be infatuated with him and – God forbid! – is threatening to elope with him if I do not grant her permission to marry. Either way, I am in danger of suffering irrecoverable loss. Would that her mother was still alive – God rest her soul – for she would, no doubt, be able to remonstrate with her. As things stand, my influence is limited, and I feel I am under the most enormous mental strain.

*Sir Charles Pomeroy's diary (22.7.1863)*

I am continuing with my plan to rid myself of the detestable

Harold; namely, to construct a pit in the wine cellar and place him therein. Indeed, I have already commissioned the work and, as part of my subterfuge, have slyly consulted Harold about my plan. My aim is to convince him that I have had a change of mind about his inheritance and his marrying Eleanor. I do not want him to suspect what is in store for him! Little does he know that a cold grave in my cellar beckons him. I do believe I have fooled him into thinking my attitude towards him has mellowed, and it makes me chuckle and snigger to see how easily he has been deceived. I worry that my facial expressions may give me away for I am losing control of my visage, at times involuntarily displaying the face of a maniac, a condition brought on by Harold's constant declarations about his right to the estate and his love for Eleanor.

*Sir Charles Pomeroy's diary (dated 26.7.1863)*

Everything is going to plan. The construction of the pit is underway, and I'm convinced that Harold has been duped into thinking my attitude towards him *has* changed. Ha, ha! Can a lamb be more easily brought to the slaughter? No doubt he has inherited a weak mind from his father (whoever *he* was), and I thank God he has no inkling of what is in store for him.

*Sir Charles Pomeroy's diary (dated 31.7.1863)*

As my plans nears fruition, I find myself sniggering more often into my handkerchief. I am amazed at my cleverness and I dance jigs in my room. I practise my snigger in front of the mirror, covering and uncovering my face with my hands. How clever of me to produce these alternate visages! It amuses me to think I can deceive onlookers, simply with a change of countenance. One moment I am the paternalistic Sir Charles, the next I am a murderer with a maniacal grin. Has this inclination existed within me all this time? Was I made this way for such a time as this? It is a question I am unable to answer. Yet I know that it is the horrible Harold who has inflicted this condition upon me! Sometimes I think I am going mad, because not even Eleanor now shows much sympathy for me.

*Sir Charles Pomeroy's diary (dated 8.8.1863)*

The pit is nearly finished and, as intended, just wide enough and long enough for Harold to lie down in. I have tried it out several times myself, being only a little shorter than the usurper, and there is three inches to spare. It will be a snug fit for him! What is more, I have decided to put a strong, sliding, metal plate over the pit to prevent him breaking out. He is powerfully built, so I need to make the pit secure. As a further precaution, I have employed builders from Northampton, 150 miles away, so they will not be around to be asked awkward questions of by the police when Harold is reported missing. What thoughts will go through Harold's mind once I have secured him in the pit? Will he imagine how long it will take him to die? Will he imagine what it is like to die of thirst and food starvation? I hope so! He has caused me to suffer, and now it is his turn!

*Sir Charles Pomeroy's diary (dated 15.8.1863)*

Today I invited the unsuspecting Harold down to the cellar, opening a bottle of my finest wine to celebrate its near completion. Believing in my change of heart, Harold complimented me on the fine masonry with which the pit had been constructed; its smooth plastered walls, and so on.

'What a marvellous wine cellar,' he congratulated.

I smiled happily. 'To your health, dear Harold!'

'To yours, dear Charles,' he added. After two bottles of wine, I began to affect a solemn posture towards him, as if sorely troubled by my previous attitude.

'I want you to know, dear Harold,' I began, 'that I have come to regard you as the rightful joint heir to my estate, and there is certainly no need for you to have recourse to the law. I have come to understand that my jealousy of you was my initial problem. I simply wanted to keep the entire estate, and Eleanor, to myself. Do forgive me, dear Harold, and if you can think of a penance, I will gladly honour it.'

On hearing these remarks, his countenance changed remarkably. For the remainder of the evening, he continued to shower me with compliments and felicitations and I went to bed convinced my plan would succeed.

The following evening, we again stood in the same place, drinking wine.

'Eleanor and I are delighted you have decided to give us your blessing, Charles. And we will be honoured and rejoice if you will join us in our nuptials.' He was certainly inebriated as he shared these sentiments, swaying backwards and forwards, spilling some of the contents of my very best wine into the pit – the drunkard. He sanctified his own grave with a claret.

'Think nothing of it!' I replied, struggling to hide a snigger, 'all that matters Harold, is that you will soon be enjoying the fruits of your inheritance; an inheritance you so richly deserve.' But it was his descent into Hades I was thinking of, and the torment of the devil. Having lulled him into a state of relaxation, I seized my opportunity. On the pretext of needing fresh glasses, I sent him upstairs to fetch them and, during his absence, poured enough hemlock into his half-full glass to render even an elephant unconscious. Gleefully I watched him drain the container and, seeing the drug take effect, he was soon so unsteady on his feet that he began to slur his words. Could my salvation be far off?

'Your health, Charles,' he toasted, extravagantly.

'And to yours, dear Harold!'

Now for my master stroke! Feigning good humour, I asked him to climb down into the pit and give me his opinion on its suitability as a receptacle for wines. He did so, willingly. The dim-witted fool!

'It would make a better grave than a receptacle for wine,' he commented.

'I could have kissed him on the cheek for that!

'Don't be silly,' I assured him. 'Surely it is not long enough for a body. Lie down in it and see for yourself.'

'Delighted!' he concurred.

I could hardly contain my elation. The intended grave fitted him perfectly.

'It does fit you well,' I said, sauntering over and looking down at him, a crowbar concealed behind my back. 'But come out of it now, Harold, and try another bottle.'

'Gladly,' he said, reaching for my hand. 'Actually, Charles,' he said, 'I'm beginning to feel quite strange.' He tried to rise but found he could not. 'Oh, my goodness. I do feel most odd!' he declared, 'that wine of yours has gone to my head – I am beginning to swoon!'

'Well, you'd better lie down again, Harold,' I teased, bringing the crowbar out from behind my back and smashing it on his head. He cried out, the blood gushing from the wound. I feared I had killed him, for this was not my intention. I wanted, rather, for him to suffer the anguish of incarceration. As he lay groaning in the pit, I gratefully observed the rise and fall of his chest. Thanks be to God. Harold was still alive after all!

'Sweet dreams, Harold,' I said, sniggering as he lay there.

My work was nearly done, or so I thought, as I slid the metal cover over him and padlocked it. I danced a little jig on the lid, rejoicing that Harold was beneath. Afterwards, I put twelve heavy cases of wine on top of the cover. Now, with Harold safely entombed, I went out, locking the cellar door behind me, intending never to return to the cellar again

How wrong I was in my assumption! For I soon became obsessed with making sure the lid of the pit had remained secure. Several times I tediously removed the wine cases to check that the padlock (the key to which I always kept on a cord around my neck) had remained fastened. Each time, I found the lock was secure and my felicity seemed assured.

As time went on, however, it became difficult to hide my glee at his passing. How I longed to openly rejoice. Yet, for Eleanor's sake, I was forced to adopt a mournful pose, for my daughter was, apparently, inconsolably distressed by Harold's disappearance.

'What a cruel blow!' I commiserated, taking the opportunity to blacken Harold's name at every opportunity. 'How could he leave you so cruelly! Were his expressions of love so shallow that he couldn't even say goodbye?' It was clear that he had simply been after her money! 'Why had I not seen through him from the beginning?' The proof, if proof were needed, was his sudden departure. 'Could anyone be sorrier than I at what had happened to her?' How cruel was fate to snatch her happiness away.

Hearing not a peep from the hated Harold, as I continued to check the cellar, the weeks passed uneventfully. Curiously, however, my daughter, contrary to her declarations, began to behave as if she did not miss him. This puzzled me greatly. Nevertheless, I continued to play my part as the loving father insisting, at great expense, that the manor and its lands be thoroughly searched, then, when nothing was found, insisted they were searched again. I ensured that ponds were dragged – in case he had fallen in and could not swim. I offered a reward for anyone able to shed light on his disappearance. Facetiously, when all my efforts had been concluded, I proffered the possible explanation that, 'Perhaps he has had another bout of amnesia!?'

But at the zenith of my self-congratulation, my conscience played a cruel trick on me. After the police had concluded their enquiries, I began to suffer recurring nightmares in which I dreamt that Harold had escaped his confinement and was roaming about the house, seeking revenge. That he sought to imprison *me* in the same way as I had *him*! Worse! He had crawled into secret passages, which, unknown to me, were under the house and was sawing through the floor joists in order that I might fall through into traps set below.

As my paranoia grew, I began to find it impossible to make the simplest of decisions about my life. Moreover, in a terrifying development, the past and the future began to merge into one. In my scheme of things, I thought I could return to childhood on a whim, or advance far into the future. The restraints of temporality disappeared. The most common sensations began to flood my mind. A dripping tap became the roar of Niagara; a ticking clock sounded like the bell of doom; the chirp of a grasshopper was like the screech of chalk on a blackboard. I became hostage to every sensory impulse, and I *imagined that* my servants were orchestrating a campaign to poison me. The proof came when I heard them scheming to put me in a mental asylum. What ingratitude!

My suspicions became facts and undeniable realities. I would go down to the cellar to see if the padlock was still fastened. I sniffed the sliding cover. There no odour emanating from his putrefying corpse. The padlock was intact, he must surely still be there! But I could not open the pit to reassure myself for, if it was found to be empty, I would lose my wits! And if he was still there, and against the odds, alive, would he not jump out, bloody-headed, and clasp me to his stinking body, drag *me* into his abode?

As my paranoia developed further: I forced my servants to taste my food; I inverted each piece of footwear, fearing a scorpion or other poisonous creature had been secreted therein. Everywhere around the hall, I had the bushes cut down, I *knew* they were being used by my servants to spy on me! Each knot of wood in the panelling was filled in to stop them spying on me from the other side. I had the floorboards taken up, at enormous cost, and replaced with new ones. I needed to be sure I would not fall through into Harold's traps. Eventually, my behaviour became so erratic and disturbed that Eleanor wrote to Garland, claiming I had gone mad, the most profound betrayal of all. In the end, Drs Crabb and Simons came to incarcerate me in Garland. They also believe I *have* gone mad, and the whole world now opposes me.

*Sir Charles Pomeroy's diary (dated 9.10.1863)*

And now, in accordance with Dr Crabb's instruction, I am temporarily returned to Chittington Manor, walking through the entrance hall closely followed by Drs Crabb and Simons. A police constable and an inspector follow. A nurse accompanies us with a syringe, to inject me if I become too troublesome. She also carries a straight-jacket. Eleanor walks in front of me and I follow in her footsteps. I will not follow in any others! I trail along after her down the steps. Why are they leading me down here? Have they discovered my crime? This is no therapy! I see the padlock on the sliding lid has been removed. How can this be? I clutch at the key which, even now, remains tied around my neck. Is someone else in possession of a key to the pit! Are they going to make me slide back the metal cover and look at Harold's putrefying corpse?! They do so, I avert my eyes. I dare not look!

'Look down!' commands Dr Crabb, forcing me to drag my eyes down to view the expected horror. I have no choice but to obey. But what is this!? Harold is not there! I hear a voice from behind me. I recognise it. It is Harold's voice!

'Yes, Charles, it is I!' I turn to see the detestable Harold in rude health, accompanied by Eleanor. 'We guessed your intentions all along, Charles, so I asked Eleanor to check the pit shortly after you had departed. Eleanor had a duplicate key made, taking the original from around your neck while you slept. It was she, and your servants, who set me free. I sustained a terrible injury at your hand, Charles, one which might have killed me. It was worth the risk to expose you as the madman and murderer that you are. You have become so accustomed to cruelty and deception, it is years since you have known yourself. Subsequent to my incarceration, both Eleanor and I went to the police. They thought it best to let you play out your little game and incriminate yourself. With the assistance of your own physician, I wrote to Dr Crabb, explaining that you had gone mad, having condemned yourself by your own actions. I was in the pit but a matter of hours before Eleanor released me and attended to my injuries. So now, Charles, you have lost not only your great estate but the love of a dear daughter, in addition to your good name and your freedom. You thought you were leading us a merry dance, Charles, but the converse was the case. Your own diaries, secured by the police, condemn you out of hand. You shall stand trial for your crimes, and in all likelihood be declared insane, for you *are* insane. But should you ever recover your wits, perhaps you will consider your wicked deeds and the lofty position you have squandered. The estate will pass to Eleanor, whom I secretly married in a private ceremony. Incidentally, Charles, I had no provable claim to your estate; no legal papers of any kind to prove my lineage and inheritance, only what my mother in St Lucia told me. In the end, I suspect you and your estate would have been quite safe. A fact you might like to think about during your unavoidably long period of incarceration in Garland. Goodbye Charles.'

*Sir Charles Pomeroy's diary (dated 09.11.1863)*

Now, I am all alone in Garland Mental Hospital, though wise to their schemes; wise to their cellar games. Let them spy on me in my cell; they'll not learn a thing! One day Chittington Manor will once again be mine. Eleanor, at least, will be pleased to see me. I will again take my revenge on the detestable Harold, for it is he who has wrought this destruction. Eleanor and the estate *are* mine and will always be mine. No-one can take them away from me! True, I made a mistake in confining Harold in the cellar. Next time, I will dig a deep mine shaft and throw him into it, sealing it over with rubble. No-one will find him then! I shall live out my days in undisturbed peace with Eleanor. They won't get the better of me again! But why can't I keep a straight face?

# The French Dolls

The twin French dolls were beautifully dressed, twelve inches tall, with large translucent blue eyes. Their lips, an unsmiling pink, pouted demurely, their blonde hair a delight. Yet, for all their attractive appearance, just an hour spent in their presence left one feeling a profound sense of unease which lingered for days.

How did they come into my possession? A Krakow dealer in figurines and mannequins got in touch with me through a London intermediary, who knew of my interest in antique or unique dolls. So it was, on 11th March 2005, that I arrived in Krakow, and booked into my hotel near the Florian Gate.

It had been a tedious journey, via Antwerp and Berlin, and I was glad to find a hotel in the Old Town. I was given a spacious, comfortable, bedroom looking out onto the Czaetoryski Museum, just around the corner from the Slowacki Theatre. The following day, I would visit Mrs Winklehorst, the Dutch lady who owned the dolls, who lived in the Kazmierz, the old Jewish Quarter of the city. I set out my dolls' case on top of the chest of drawers, convinced it would soon be hosting the French dolls. Hungry after my long journey, for dinner I enjoyed an unusually fine piece of pork, pickled viands and various hors d'oeuvres.

In the morning, finding time on my hands, I took the opportunity to walk around Rynek Glowny and the Cloth Hall, before drifting into Grodza Street, where I caught the tram destined for Stradomska and Krakowska, disembarking near Jozefa Street in the Jewish Quarter. As I headed for Mrs Winklehorst's house, an old Jewish man followed me past the rather sombre building. He later proved to be the woman's husband. The atmosphere of the district was unrelentingly gloomy, perhaps because, during the Second World War, the Kazmierz district had been home to some sixty thousand Jews. These poor people never recovered from Hitler's virulent anti-Semitic drive through Poland, which took the greatest proportion of them to concentration and extermination camps, notably Auschwitz. And not only the Jews, but non-Jewish Poles and Russian prisoners; in fact, anybody, including priests and the Polish intelligentsia, who Hitler thought might pose a threat to the Third Reich. As everyone knows, Auschwitz was the most infamous Polish camp of all, notorious for its recreational murder and brutality. Now, in the Kazmierz district, live only a handful of the people of the Old Covenant, ghosts of happier times whose sadness and despondency oozed from the fabric of the buildings as I passed by.

At the door of my destination in Pozan Street, I raised and let go of the doorknocker. Almost immediately, the old man who had been trailing behind me, came up and tapped me on the shoulder, explaining that I was knocking on the door of his wife's house. He produced a key, turned it in the lock, and the door swung open. Ushering me inside, we proceeded along a dimly lit, green-tiled, corridor giving way to orange and cream wallpaper stained with damp and, in places, lifting off the walls. A small strip of brown carpet ran down the centre of the hall, clashing with the green tiles. Turning to the right, we entered a sparsely furnished room in which sat an old, red-faced woman with greying hair, nursing the French dolls in her lap. She wore a scruffy, flowery dress with stars printed upon it – a concession to being Jewish? I had only just sat down when the large, noisily ticking, cuckoo clock opposite struck the hour. Emerging from it, instead of the proverbial cuckoo, erupted a butcher with a meat cleaver, chasing a young woman. This fellow, wearing the grin of an imbecile, was followed by a small boy trundling a wheelbarrow containing severed heads. It was clear by his performance that the butcher intended the woman's head to join those already in the wheelbarrow. Round and round they went, the butcher's cleaver rising and falling as the cuckoo called unseen, intent on his grisly mission. After what seemed an eternity, but what could have been little longer than a minute, the butcher gave a disembodied 'yo-ho-ho', and the mechanism clanked to a stop, all three characters disappearing inside. The old woman chuckled, pleased with the display, though it was certainly not to my taste.

'You are Mr Raymond?' she enquired. 'You've come to see the dolls?'

'Yes,' I replied, still wondering at the clock's gruesome merry-go-round.

She explained that the dolls had once belonged to two little twin Jewish girls living near the town of Bonnevai, not far from Paris, who had disappeared days before the end of the Second World War. The dolls had been found by a kind neighbour, who had held on to them in case the girls returned. But the girls were never seen again. The following day their mother was also taken by the Vichy.

'To cut a long story short,' she said, 'the twin girls had been picked up by the Vichy Gendarme and sent to Auschwitz concentration camp. It was a tragedy but, as you can see, they've been kept in remarkably good condition and haven't been damaged.' She looked at me keenly, hoping her tale was striking the appropriate connection between their condition and price. She continued: 'The neighbour into whose possession the dolls had fallen, married a Polish man who still lives here in the Jewish Quarter. I bought them in the local market.' She held the dolls out in front of her, inviting me to take them.

'They *do* look beautiful,' I said, placing them on my lap.

The old man nodded silently.

I saw they were in completely original condition, made in about 1930. I could not make out the name of the manufacturer but they were typical of dolls made in Marseilles before the war. They wore short, puffed-sleeve, dresses with beautiful white buttons fastening up to the neck. Their eyes, whether from some manufacturing defect or other cause, looked haunted, and their expression seemed to change from moment to moment. Had they knowledge of the horror the girls had experienced in Auschwitz? Had what had happened to the girls somehow been transmitted to them? Sceptics may scoff at such a suggestion, but I knew from my travels around the world that many people believe artefacts and effigies of the dead can absorb aspects of the memories of their ancestors. As I looked into their eyes, I became convinced that the dolls had knowledge of the girls' fate, and the dolls seemed to vibrate in my hands, as if they knew of their owners' horrific experiences in the camp. Was I imagining that their cheeks reddened as I held them?

Feeling strangely afraid, I handed them back to Mrs Winklehorst, thinking that she had not fully taken me entirely into her confidence about the dolls, and that some evil had entered the figurines. Nevertheless, I offered, and Mrs Winklehorst quickly accepted, the sum of fifty pounds for them. I knew they were probably worth far more. However, business, as they say, is business, so I went out into the hall having packed the dolls in the carrying case. At the threshold of the door, Mr Winklehorst put his hand on my shoulder, at length explaining that Mrs Winklehorst attended a nearby spiritualist church, at which, during a lively session, a medium had passed on all kinds of horrors about what had happened to the girls in the camp and that, subsequently, his wife had not been able to sleep at night, haunted by their history. He said that an inmate who had survived Auschwitz, where the girls had met their fate, and who also attended the spiritualist church, had spoken with the girls as he had entered a trance, just as they had entered the gas chamber. The girls being twins, he said, they had been subject to the diabolical experiments of Dr Mengele, the *Schtzstaffel* officer in the camp. Mrs Winklehorst had seen the dolls walking about the house at night, and more than once they had come into her room and bitten her on the hand while she'd slept. He confessed that neither he nor his wife had had a moment's peace since the dolls had come into the house, and he was glad they were being taken.

'My wife believes the dolls absorbed the horrors of what the girls endured at Auschwitz,' he said. 'How, I don't know.' The look of fear in his eyes was not easily forgotten. I wondered at the influence of the dolls upon his wife's mental state.

Returning past the sombre buildings to reach the end of Grodza Street, I boarded a convenient tram to the city centre. Later, as I sat having my dinner in the Planty, across from the Colleguin Movum, I decided I would sell the dolls on as soon as possible. Suddenly I was surrounded by a gaggle of university students, one of whom told me how remorseful the Germans now were at the actions of the Nazis in Poland, explaining that a young German student, just recently, had been beaten senseless by a gang of Polish youths chanting 'Nazi! Nazi!' A little while later, finding the bar disappointingly empty, I retired to my room, but not before taking a message left in reception by an English customer interested in purchasing the dolls. A handsome profit seemed to be in the offing!

Imagine my surprise when, upon entering the room, vacated but an hour earlier, I found one of the dolls in a sitting position, resting its back against the case lid. The other was standing upright, its arms outstretched, as if it was heading for the door. Had someone been examining them in my absence? Since the bed covers had not been turned down, or the towels replaced, I phoned reception. They confirmed that no-one had been in to service the room. How then was I to explain the dolls' change of position? Was I to believe that the dolls could self-animate? Such a proposition seemed preposterous, as I again laid them side by side in the case, this time locking the lid. I read for a while, before switching off the light and must have fallen asleep. I cannot describe the horror I felt when, in that strange state between sleep and waking, I found the dolls lying adjacent to my pillowed head, their faces towards me, warm puffs of air exhaling from them onto my cheeks. In the next instant, I felt their painful bites. 'What's this!!' I cried out loud, climbing out of bed and wiping away the blood that trickled down either side of my chin. Turned onto their backs, the dolls were looking up at me. Was there a suspicious smile on their lips? I grabbed them roughly and threw them into the dolls' case, again locking it securely. But what was the use? They were obviously able to open the case themselves.

When I awoke the following morning, I half wondered if I had dreamt the whole thing, or had fallen into a kind of delirium, but for the evidence of the blood-stained tissue in the waste bin with which I had wiped my cheeks.

On the return journey to London, I ensured that the case containing the dolls was kept securely locked in the overhead rack and, upon arrival in London, I quickly took them round to the interested client, relieving him of a considerable sum of money. I was honest enough to recount to him what had happened to me in Krakow, concerning the dolls, though he seemed to be in no doubt I was a victim of my own imagination.

Later, I heard that this same client, a Mr Robert Lim, had been found dead on his lounge floor, his face thought to have been bitten by rats, or else attacked by a cat. Whether or not it was a domestic, or a wild creature, his face was so badly rent as to be unrecognisable. Evidence of neither could be found and I can only say, I was glad that I had not held on to the dolls.

# Otto

Not long after the end of the First World War, Corporal Davison, who had served with an artillery battery during the conflict, near Geluveld, Flanders, decided to revisit the area. I suppose he was probably justifiably proud of the part he had played in the war and wanted to see the area in more normal times. Unfortunately, there are risks to retracing one's footsteps.

As a young man, the war had given him a sense of purpose and achievement which, after being demobbed, he had not regained. Now, as the train crossed Belgium towards Flanders, gazing out over the fields of poppies, he was reminded of the time when the blasted front line had been strewn with them, a symbolic memorial to the dead. The more disturbed and ravaged the battlefield, the more the poppies seemed to flourish; as if Nature herself had her own way of remembering the dead, blooming in sympathy with the carnage. Seeing them again brought sadness as he remembered his fallen comrades.

Davison's job, during the conflict, involved using his Plessy sound-ranging equipment to detect the location of German batteries. He achieved this by placing pairs of microphones at various intervals near the German lines, so giving him a bearing on the German artillery positions. He could then accurately direct British fire at the German positions. Often, he'd wondered, with some regret, how many German soldiers had been killed as a result of his work.

But our story centres on one particular day in 1915, when two young soldiers from the Rhineland, Otto and Hans, on duty together in their trench, received an incoming shell from the British artillery directed by Corporal Davison's sound detection equipment. The shell blew poor Hans to pieces. He died instantly, leaving Otto only slightly injured, though he lost consciousness. Otto was taken to a German field hospital and, though he eventually returned to the front line, he grieved daily for Hans, swearing on his life to avenge Hans's death. Eventually, Otto himself was shot by a soldier from the Royal Field Artillery but, as his lifeblood drained away, he continued to swear vengeance on Hans's killer.

After Otto's death, revenge seemed impossible, yet Otto's spirit, tormented by the death of his friend, could find no resting place. Throughout the rest of the war, in the vicinity of Flanders, Otto's ghost was regularly seen searching for the British soldier who had been instrumental in Hans's death, the very same Corporal Davison. Indeed, Otto became known as the Ghost of Geluveld. Those who saw him were so terrified by his visage that they fled, risking German bullets rather than make his acquaintance. Witnesses said that half of Otto's skull was missing, that daylight could be seen through it, and they swore that his remaining eye and a portion of his face was so terrifying to look upon, and so malignant in its expression, that even sober men became mentally unhinged at the sight of him. It was as if they had become shell-shocked, and more than one soldier completely lost his wits. Oddly, though Otto's left leg was completely absent, it seemed not to affect his locomotion, as he walked normally – just as if his missing left leg was still attached. His phantom arm continued to hold his rifle. Otto's favourite haunt was the artillery batteries around the wooded hill where Corporal Davison had operated the Plessy range-finder. As the war dragged on, Otto continued to make his regular appearances in the British trenches.

When hostilities ceased, the local inhabitants hoped that Otto would return to his home to the Rhineland. Instead, he appeared with undiminished frequency, and more intrusively, entering inhabited homes as well as derelict buildings. The inhabitants of Geluveld became convinced that Otto was still seeking to avenge Hans's death, and Mrs Jennette, with whom Davison had arranged to stay, often observed Otto's ghostly comings and goings. She would not, however, have had the courage to face the spectre, always keeping a safe distance.

'There's Otto again, Pierre,' she would say to her husband, who always affected disinterest in the ghost. 'He looks like a man starving to death, or dying of thirst, or gone mad. I swear I can hear him grinding his teeth!'

Said Pierre, 'I can sometimes hear the slap of his boots at night, as if he's walking in deep mud in the former battlefields. Doesn't he know there are only green fields there now? What a noise he makes! Spirits are supposed to be quiet, creepy things, aren't they?'

'He's a big man,' said his wife, 'at least six feet tall,' not fully understanding the implications of her husband's question. 'But who's that knocking on our door?'

It was her expected guest, the same Corporal Davison who had operated the Plessy range finder, who had arranged to stay with her while visiting his old battlefield location.

'Oh... do come in,' invited Mrs Jennette, smiling, 'We've been expecting you.' She took his coat and hung it on a peg in the hall. 'Your bed is made up and we've been able to give you a room with your requested view of the wooded area where you operated your equipment.'

'Thank you,' said Davison, going upstairs and dropping his case onto the bed. He peered out of the window at the wooded hill, his blood tingling at the thought of visiting his operation ground the following day.

'I hope you'll find the room comfortable,' said Mrs Jennette, as Davison came back downstairs. 'You'll soon discover that there's not much left of the battlefield nowadays, just the remains of a few collapsed trenches and the odd stone wall. Have you brought your range finder with you?'

'Yes,' said Corporal Davison, a man of medium height with a boyish face. 'I thought I'd set it up in the same familiar spot, to see if it can pick up any sounds, as in the days of battle. For me it will just be an exercise in nostalgia, and I'll probably leave it there when I return home, a sort of memorial to those of my comrades who died fighting the Germans and, I like to think, to the Germans themselves. There are good and bad on both sides, and I hold no animosity towards the Germans. I hope this visit will put the war to rest for me, as I really don't want to remember it at all now, yet, somehow, I feel I must visit the area again to forget it. Does that make sense to you, Mrs Jeanette?'

Mrs Jennette cocked her head to one side. 'I can understand that,' she said. 'I was in the war myself. I expect you need to get it out of your system. Doesn't he, Pierre?'

Davison heard a cough.

'I'd say so,' replied her husband.

Mrs Jennette then warned him not to be surprised if he met Otto, the German soldier.

'He's still wandering about out there, looking for someone.' She stood back and said: 'They say he's searching for the man who killed a fallen comrade, I hope it's not you he's looking for!'

'Otto? Is he still a German soldier?' asked Davison, puzzled. 'What is he doing here, is *he* staying with you?'

'No, no!' Mrs Jennette laughed. 'Otto is keeping the dead company. He's a ghost. But you don't want to meet *him!* He puts the fear of God into anyone who does. He's a ghost in a German uniform who was killed during the war. That's who Otto is!'

'You certainly *don't* want to meet him!' her husband put in. 'One glimpse is enough to last a lifetime!'

After supper, Davison went to bed thinking about ghosts. He wondered if there were such things, and consequently, he slept badly. During the night, he had a strange feeling someone was standing by his wardrobe, observing him. But, after breakfast, he trudged with his equipment up the hill, nostalgically dressed in his corporal's uniform, and placed the microphones as he had done during the conflict. Afterwards, he put on the set's headphones, sitting in a little folding chair Mrs Jennette had loaned him for his reconnaissance, periodically scanning the hinterland with his binoculars.

He did not know exactly *what* he expected to hear through the headphones, though it certainly wasn't the sound of a battle. Yet that is exactly what he *did* hear! And not in a subdued or artificial way; that would have been bad enough! No! He felt the full blast of the detonations and the roar and din of the conflict. He could smell the cordite blown across the former battlefield, and he could hear the 'whoomph!' of the batteries, and the scream of shells flying overhead. Time seemed to slip back again to 1915, and Davison found himself fully involved in the conflict again. In a lull in the bombardment, he heard a German voice calling, 'Hans, Hans… where are you…?' As far as he could understand, Hans had been killed by a detonating shell, undoubtedly one that he had directed. Now someone called Otto was swearing revenge on whoever had focused the artillery onto Otto's position. Davison wondered if he was witnessing a military exercise in the vicinity? The curious thing was, when he took off the Plessy's headphones, the noise of battle ceased abruptly and he could hear again the usual sounds of the countryside. Yet when he put them on again, the battle resumed, and the headphones produced the exact same result as before. It was as if the Plessy was communicating the past conflict directly to him, and he was at a loss as to how to explain it. Shocked and bewildered, he switched off the Plessy, leaving everything in place, and descended the hill to Mrs Jennette's. He went upstairs and, lying on his bed, greatly troubled, he dozed off. Two hours later, he heard the gong sound for dinner. Going downstairs, he asked Mrs Jeanette if she knew of any military activities taking place that day. She did not, adding that any training exercises were normally carried out many miles away.

Mrs Jeanette registered Davison's low mood over dinner, commenting; 'You *do* look so very pale this evening, Mr Davison. Have you had a fright of some kind? Did you see Otto up on the hill? He is often seen there. Has he frightened you?'

'You mean the German ghost?' asked Davison, rather irritated. 'No, I haven't seen a ghost, Mrs Jennette, but I did hear the sound of a battle just as if it was yesterday. That's why I wanted to know if there had been any military exercises nearby. I cannot fathom out what happened to me. It was just like I was back in the conflict.

'Well, when he appears,' she said, ignoring Davison's report, 'you'll recognise him, that's for sure. He is still wearing his German uniform and will be carrying his rifle. He has a leg and an arm missing. Oh! And half his face is missing as well. He does examine you with a dreadful scrutiny. I shouldn't want to meet up with him. Neither would I want to be the one he's, apparently, looking for. Watch out Mr Davison!

The following day, feeling that he needed some normal, everyday experience to restore his nerves, he went into Ypres and visited St George's Chapel, saying prayers for his fallen comrades. He found the town little changed, and he easily recognised several landmarks. He was pleased to discover a small museum, with a battlefield display model of the German, British, and French positions during the war. After idly examining the artefacts, he became interested in an incongruous, life-sized model of a German soldier, standing in a corner of the museum, leaning with a bayoneted rifle over the parapet of a mock trench. The helmet covered most of the German's blond hair. Davison thought the blue eyes were particularly realistic, which he thought were probably made from semi-precious stones, which gave them a particularly intense, translucent quality, as if they were actually registering what they were seeing. *How ridiculous*, thought Davison, as the soldier's eyes seemed to follow him about the room. He felt so uncomfortable that he hid behind an exhibit for a while, only to find, when he did emerge that the hairs on the back of his neck were standing up, and the dummy was still looking at him. Exiting the room, he told himself *It's only a dummy!*

Back at his lodgings, he asked Mrs Jennette if she had visited the museum and, in particular, had noticed the German soldier in the exhibit. She said that she had, that the name of the model of the German soldier was Otto, so-called because of the ghost of the German soldier who haunted the area. Davison recounted how the dummy's eyes seemed to follow him around the room. 'It made me feel most peculiar. Did it make you feel that way, Mrs Jennette?'

'No. I really can't say that it did,' she replied. 'Mr Davison, it's only a dummy!'

The following morning, Davison again took his little folding chair up the hill hoping, as he walked through the dark twiggy woods, that his experience of the previous day would not be repeated. He now felt, rather than putting the conflict to rest, he was being invited to live it all over again, and it was with a rather dreadful reluctance that he put on the headphones, only to hear, as on the previous day, the sound of the battle raging. He heard Otto sobbing, grieving for his fallen comrade, and swearing to take vengeance on the soldier responsible for Hans's death. Davison wanted to put down the headphones for ever, but curiosity kept them glued to his ears. He then lost track of the time since he had climbed up the hill.

More-or-less, half an hour before he intended to return to Mrs Jeanette's, a patchy fog began to descend and a light rain began to fall. Through his binoculars he glimpsed the figure of a blond-haired German soldier, in uniform, climbing up to his position. In a matter of minutes, he saw that it had the same penetrating blue eyes, helmet and insignia as the solider seen the day before in the Ypres museum. The eyes had the same intense, translucent, quality that made them seem alive. He noticed that part of the soldier's face was missing, and one arm and most of one leg. He knew, from what Mrs Jeanette had told him, it was the ghost of Otto. Davison's heart leapt into his mouth and he wanted to run. Yet, fascinated, something kept him rooted to the spot. Otto came within a few feet of him, and looked directly at him. Davison saw there were beetles and worms crawling out of his mouth, flies buzzing about his injured limbs. At last, self-preservation kicked in, and Davison began to back away, his Plessy headphones inadvertently detaching themselves. 'My God, this is actually happening!' he cried out, but the soldier came on, thrusting with his bayonet.

It would not at this point have done much good to tell Davison that he was being confronted by a ghost; or to postulate that the incorporeal were not usually in a position to harm the living. From Davison's point of view, Otto *was* real; as real as the bayoneted rifle he held in his hand. Davison watched, horrified, as Otto's blue eyes vanished from their sockets, and his mouth became a teeming void. Even the flesh and muscle on Otto's good arm and leg were transformed into bony appendages, to be horribly replaced by metacarpals and metatarsals. What confronted Davison now, was as a walking skeleton. He wanted to scream the loudest scream that had ever been heard upon a battlefield, but found he could not. In the next instant, Otto sprang forward and thrust his bayonet deep into Davison's abdomen, his grinning jaw pleased with the fountain of blood issuing from Davison's wound. Now Davison managed to utter the scream his lungs had been preparing for, and it rippled terrifyingly, through the woods. The birds, previously silent, began to chirp again as Otto toppled backwards landing parallel with Davison's own dying body, its right arm falling across Davison's chest; as if, in death, they had become bosom buddies, their sightless eyes staring up at the Flanders sky.

At dinner time, and after some fruitless calling, Mrs Jennette went up the hill and found Davison's body next to the skeletal remains of a German soldier. Shocked to the core, she ran home and called the gendarme, who came on the scene commendably quickly. The duty medical officer did not know what to make of the scene, but called an ambulance to take Davison's body to the local morgue. They thought Davison had been killed by some local youths, though there was no evidence of such, and nothing was found to have been stolen from his person.

After Davison's death, Otto's appearances became less frequent until, some years later, they ceased altogether. Davison's body and his belongings were returned to England, and Mr and Mrs Jennette considered the episode closed. Though, for some time after, Mrs Jeanette had trouble with her nerves.

'Poor Mr Davison,' she said to her husband, some weeks afterwards, 'Fancy surviving the war only to be killed by the bayonet of a German rifle in peacetime. Yet it's an odd thing for Davison to have done, to have gone up there to play with his range finder, so long after the war has ended, don't you think? It's just asking for trouble.'

'Well,' said Mr Jennette, tapping out his pipe on the hearth. 'Whether or not he was asking for trouble, he certainly found it. But I think you're right. It's not a good idea to try and act out the past so long after the event.'

I should add that I stayed with Mrs Jennette some time after Davison had left. The sound-ranging detecting equipment belonging to Davison remains to this day on top of the wooded hill. Mrs Jennette once thought to retrieve it, but held back from doing so on account of what had happened to Davison. I also visited the Ypres museum, and was told by the curator that the mannequin, once an exhibit in the museum, had been found on the hill next to where Davison's body had been discovered. It was returned, he told me, and the mannequin still languishes in a cupboard in the museum.

# Mad Allen

Near the cathedral, by the river, Cecil Hungerford walked that autumnal day, through the beech leaves which lay thick on the path to the old ruined hermitage. A mad monk, or at least he was held to be mad locally, had taken up residence in the hermitage in 1830. Though he was given the nickname, Mad Allen, this epithet did not detract from his reputation as a soothsayer, frequently consulted, as he was, by the local nobility, including Sir Humphrey Digbarton, on whose estate the hermitage was located.

At first Allen resided there peacefully. The trouble came when Sir Humphrey's youngest daughter, Charlotte, the undisputed beauty of the county, became a close friend of Allen's. Initially, the baronet, possessed of a romantic spirit, was rather taken with the idea of a hermit living on his land, after the fashion of the time, but became less pleased with his daughter's developing affections for Allen.

It was known that Mad Allen had been a landed gentleman – a Welshman, swindled out of his estate by his younger brother, Charles. To make matters worse, his faithless wife had been complicit in the swindle and had run off with the said Charles, a womaniser of some notoriety. Neither of the parties were seen again.

Understandably, perhaps, Allen began to despair of life, retreating into the arms of laudanum and Mother Nature until, wandering onto Sir Humphrey's estate, he began to invoke the woodland spirits. Visitors to the estate observed him jumping and leaping about in the woods, reciting strange incantations, and shaking his rattle at them. It was not long before an extensive folklore grew up about him. And Allen was credited with the ability to call down wind and rain, cure sickness in animals and restore fertility in cattle. He had an uncanny ability to predict the weather – particularly the onset and termination of the seasons – and around his waist hung bones of various animals marked with strange symbols, and around his neck he kept a gourd containing "who knew what?". This he would remove and shake at passers-by, frightening them half out of their wits, and often, so badly that they never set foot in the woods again.

The only person who could settle him was Sir Humphrey's daughter, Charlotte, herself a lover of nature and a regular visitor to the hermitage. Her presence had a remarkable calming effect on Allen, as she sat quietly at his feet, providing him with food and wine. It seemed there was something about her that reminded him of his faithless wife, Florence who, though she had betrayed him comprehensively, was still fondly remembered by the soothsayer. For her part, Charlotte felt her feelings for him running deep, nurtured by his empathic understanding of nature.

'Birds and trees and animals harm no-one,' was his oft-repeated phrase to her, and he prophesied that, 'One day I shall truly be at one with them, and I will that my bones to be laid in a secret place prepared beforehand.' He took her to a small cavern hidden away in a wooded recess in his rocky domain, containing a stone sarcophagus 'There,' he said, showing her his intended resting place. 'When I'm dead, you shall slide this stone cover over me, being careful to keep the gourd in place around my neck, as it protects me, and a curse on anyone who disturbs my rest.' As if in confirmation of his oath, a sudden gust of leaves blew into the cave, swirling a multitude of leaves around her head and shoulders.

'Oh!' she cried, 'the leaves have a mind of their own!' alarmed as they circled thicker and faster around her head.

Allen stepped forward and muttered a strange incantation: 'There,' he said, shaking the gourd at them, 'Be gone!' and the vortex subsided.

One bright day, Charlotte asked him: 'Don't you ever wish to return to your former life? The life you've left behind?' She smiled, stroking his hand, searching the steel-blue eyes that held her gaze. She wished with all her heart to restore him to society.

'I'll soon be done with life,' he said, thoughtfully. 'This is all I want now.' He took her hand. 'This, and you are all I need.' He gazed into the middle distance, and she knew Allen's words were final and would never be retracted.

During the years that passed, Charlotte and Allen delighted in each other's company, Allen promising that death would not be the end of their affections. When his spirit finally departed, she wept bitterly and, as promised, recruited two servants from the hall to place him in the sarcophagus in the cave he had previously shown her. As they slid the heavy stone lid over him, she made the servants swear to keep his whereabouts secret, cautioning them that Allen's curse would rest upon anyone who disturbed his burial place, with a power she herself had seen. And the secret *was* kept until Cecil Hungerford, one of the retainers who had helped Allen into his sarcophagus, came tramping through the leaves to the hermitage on that fateful day. For Hungerford, dismissed from his duties at the hall for reason of sloth, and bearing a grievance against Sir Humphrey, sought to relieve Allen's sarcophagus of any valuables contained therein. He did not believe in Allen's curse and imagined that Charlotte might have placed a valuable trinket, or other such token of her affection, therein.

In a drunken boast in the King's Arms, the previous evening, Hungerford had bragged to the landlord, 'I have no fear of Mad Allen. I had no fear of him when he was alive! Many, on account of him are too afraid to set foot in those woods, particularly Molly Robinson who came out white-faced and talking gibberish, but *I'll* never admit to being frightened of a ghost!'

Determined to violate Mad Allen's resting place, ignoring the curse, he went armed with a crowbar into the secret chamber containing Allen's coffin, levering the stone lid until it slid free and crashed to the floor. By the light of his candle, he surveyed Allen's remains. He saw the putrefying eyes staring up at him, the bony jaw gaping almost fully open, the suspiciously lingering smile upon what remained of the soothsayer's lips. In a sudden movement, the index finger of Allen's left hand pointed up to him accusingly. '*What's this!*' he cried, shocked. Undeterred, he soon continued searching both the coffin and the cave, though he found nothing of value in either. In a final act of desecration, he unfastened the gourd from around Allen's neck, remembering that Charlotte said it possessed magical properties and, fastening it around his own, planned to have some sport with it among the trees and test its power.

He had not retreated far back on the path through the woods, when he began to agitate the gourd in the manner Charlotte had described from her observation of Allen, following this up with some incantations of his own making, dancing around in mock ritual, jerking the gourd this way and that, kicking up the leaves with his shoes and shouting, '*Perform!*'

At first, there was no perceptible effect, and he thought to smash the gourd against a tree. But, at that instant, a flurry of leaves from the many thousands littering the forest floor flew up and began to circle around his head. Thicker and thicker, faster and faster, they flew until they began to stick to his face, eyes, and mouth. Soon he could no longer see. In the next instant, he heard an incantation in Allen's own voice and found himself in a veritable tornado of leaves. The leaves flew around him so thick that his whole body was soon completely covered. He struggled to free himself, twisting this way and that, rubbing himself like an animal on the lower branches of a tree. In vain he tried to rid himself of the suffocating mass, shouting and crying out that he had meant no harm, begging Allen for forgiveness. Alas, there was no-one to hear him. The depth of leaves increased until he was completely cocooned, just as the larvae of a developing insect is cocooned before its metamorphosis. Unfortunately, there was to be no second life for Hungerford. Asphyxiated, he toppled over and rolled down the bank into the river, the air in the leaves keeping him afloat as the current conveyed his corpse downstream. When it touched the sacred ground of the cathedral, the leaves flew away and his body sank beneath the water, never to be seen again. A while later, downstream, the gourd floated free to the surface and was retrieved, by chance, by Charlotte's maidservant who took it to her mistress reposing at her dressing table. Recognising the gourd at once, Charlotte clasped it to her bosom, and jumped up, exclaiming, 'Allen! What has happened to you!!' Knowing the gourd must have been stolen; on the following stormy day when the leaves thrashed wildly in the trees, she was drawn outside by a strange impulse. Almost immediately hearing Allen's voice, she placed the gourd around her neck and went out into the maelstrom. Her maid saw the leaves swirling round her, hearing her conversing with someone she could not see. Charlotte headed for the hermitage, followed by her servant, watching her laughing and smiling, the leaves flying around her. Now the whole forest erupted, a curtain of leaves inserted itself between Charlotte and herself. When it subsided, Charlotte had vanished and, though the maid searched in vain for her, eventually she returned tearfully to the hall and reported what she had witnessed to Sir Humphrey.

The grieving baronet, distraught, searched for his daughter for many years, making excavations in the woods where Mad Allen had resided. No trace of his beloved was ever found. Exhausted and grief-stricken, Sir Humphrey's physician commanded him to rest. He spent his remaining years pining for his lost daughter. Alas, just before his death, the hermitage was lost forever beneath a landslide.

The woods and cliffs remain, to this day, the haunt of ravens and owls. On windy days, when yellow and brown leaves scuttle merrily along the path, leaves can be seen swirling by the river. If the wind is very high, there may also be seen a well-dressed lady and a poor-looking gentleman strolling hand in hand together.